Charles A Federer

The Ballad of Flodden Field

A Poem of the XVIth Century

Charles A Federer

The Ballad of Flodden Field
A Poem of the XVIth Century

ISBN/EAN: 9783744786621

Printed in Europe, USA, Canada, Australia, Japan

Cover: Foto ©Andreas Hilbeck / pixelio.de

More available books at **www.hansebooks.com**

The Ballad

OF

FLODDEN FIELD,

A Poem of the XVIth Century.

EDITED BY

CHARLES A. FEDERER, L.C.P.

Manchester:

HENRY GRAY, ANTIQUARIAN & TOPOGRAPHICAL PUBLISHER,
25, CATHEDRAL YARD.
1884.

BRADFORD:

JOHN S. TOOTHILL, PRINTER, 93, UPPER GODWIN STREET.

Contents:

The Famous History or Ballad

OF THE

BATTLES FOUGHT IN FLODDON FIELD,[1]

Taken from an
Ancient Manuscript which was transcribed by
Mr. Richard Guy,
late Schoolmaster in Ingleton, Yorkshire.[2]

Part I.

THE FIRST FIT.

(To a pleasant Tune.)

Now will I ceafe here to recite   1
    The King's[3] affairs in France fo wide,
And of domeftick jars I'll write,
    That in his abfence did betide.
A fearful field in verfe I'll frame,   2
    If you'll be pleafed to underftand :
O Floddon Mount![4] thy wond'rous name
    Doth fore affright my trembling hand.
Thou God of War! do me admit   3
    For to difcourfe with founding praife
This bloody field, this fearful fight,
    Fought in our old forefathers' days !

Pardon, ye poets all, I cry,   4
   My fimple, rude, and rugged rhyme,
Ev'n though the hill Parnaffus high
   Prefumptuoufly I prefs to climb!
For what is he, with haughty ftyle   5
   Such deeds of honour could contrive?
No, not the learned Virgil great,
   If that on earth he was alive,
That could reveal in volume fhort   6
   Great Howard's³ deeds who did excell.
Though lovely print made no report,
   Fame would not fail the fame to tell.
Or thou, O Stanley,⁶ wondrous man!   7
   Thou fon of Mars! who can proclaim
Thy matchlefs deeds?   Tell me who can
   Paint thy juft praife on wings of fame?
Thy doleful daywork ftill fhall be   8
   In Scotland curf'd with an outcry :
For Hector's match this man was he,
   Who climbed the mount of Floddon high.
What banners bravely blaz'd and borne!   9
   What ftandards ftout brought to the ground!
What worthy lords by him forlorne,
   That forrow in Scotland yet doth found!
Ye heav'nly powers! your aid I crave!   10
   My flender mufe help to awake;
Grant of this work, in hand I have,
   A fine and lucky end may make!

Before King Henry croſt the ſeas,   11
    And e'er to France he did transfleet,
He thought the Scots might him diſeaſe
    With conſtituted captains meet.
He knew that Engliſh Kings they fought,   12
    And by what might they were controul'd ;
Much more he in their abſence thought
    What damage had been done of old.
And leaſt that they ſhould work ſome teene, 13
    As they thought to have done indeed,
He left his realm unto his queene
    For to be ruled as there was need ;
Then for the earl of Surrey⁵ ſent,   14
    And regent of the North him made,
And bad him, " If the Scots were bent
    " The northern borders to invade :
" That he ſhould raiſe a royal band   15
    " In Biſhoprick⁷ and in Yorkſhire,
" In Weſtmorcland and Cumberland,
    " In Cheſhire and in Lancaſhire.
" And if thou need Northumberland,"   16
    Quoth he, " there be ſtrong men and ſtout
" That will not ſtick, if need they ſtand,
    " To fight on horſeback or on foot.
" There is the valiant Dacres⁸ old,   17
    " Warden of the Weſt march is he ;
" There are the bows of Kendal bold,
    " Who fierce will fight and never flee.

" There is Sir Edward Stanley ſtout,   18
   " For martial ſkill clear without mack,
" Of Lathom houſe⁹ by line come out,¹⁰
   " Whoſe blood will never turn their back :
" All Lancaſhire will live and die   19
   " With him, ſo chiefly will Cheſhire :
" For through his father's force," quoth he,
   " This kingdom firſt came to my fire."¹²
" Lord Clifford¹¹ too, a luſty troope   20
   " Will there conduct, a captain wise ;
" And with the luſty knight, lord Scroope,¹³
   " The power of Richmondſhire will riſe.
" The wardens all look that you warn   21
   " To hearken what the Scots forecaſt,
" And if they ſigns of war diſcern,
   " Bid them the beacons fire faſt."
The earl then with a ſorry heart   22
   Had drowned his face with trickling tears,
When from his prince he did depart,
   And from his royal country peers.
" And thou," quoth he, " Almighty God,   23
   " Let him a death moſt ſhameful dye
" Which is the cauſe of mine abode,
   " Bereav'd of my king's company !"
Some tho't to th' king of Scots that he   24
   Did wiſh ſuch ſad untimely fate,
And ſome to the earl of Derby¹⁴
   With whom he had a great debate.

The earl did then his tenants all   25
   In musters fair and brave elect,
And on his way, by journeys small,
   To Pomfret castle did direct.
Then did he send Sir William Bulmer[15]   26
   And bad him on the borders lye,
With ordinance and other geer
   Each house of fence[16] to fortify.
And bad him call the borderers bould,   27
   And hold with him in readiness,
And get him word with speed he could,
   If that the Scots meant his distress.
Then cauf'd he watch in every street,   28
   And posts to run thro' downs and dales ;
So what was wrought, he knew of it,
   From Carlisle to the coast of Wales.
When flying fame, that monstrous wight,   29
   With hundred wings was nimbly flown,
And in the court of Scotland light,
   And all abroad was blaz'd and blown,
Of great King Henry's enterprize,   30
   And how he forc'd was into France[17]
With all his peers, in princely wise,
   To bring that land to complaisance :
England to over-run with rage   31
   The Scots then meant, as was their guise.
Still as the king was under age,
   Or occupy'd some other wise,

King James's[18] courage did increafe,   32
  And of his counfel crav'd to know
If he had better live in peace,
  Or fight againft his brother-in-law ?
" Alas !" faid he, " my heart is fore,   33
  " And care conftraineth me to weep,
" That ever I to England fwore
  " A league or love a day to keep.
" Had I not entred in that band,   34
  " I fwear now by this burnifh'd blade.
" England and Scotland both one land
  " And kingdom one I could have made.
" That realm we foon fhould over-run,   35
  " That England, when this age is past,
" As to our elders they have done,
  " Should homage do us to the laft."
Then ftood there up a baron ftout,   36
  The lufty lord of Douglas[19] blood,
" My liege," quoth he, " have you no doubt,
  " But mark my words with mirthful mood.
" The league is broke, no doubt you need,   37
  " Believe me, liege, my words are true.
" What was the Englifh Admiral's[20] deed,
  " When Andrew Barton[21] bold he flew ?
" Your fhips and armour too he took,   38
  " And fince, their king did nothing fear
" To fend his aid againft the duke
  " Of Gelders,[22] your own coufin dear.

" Hath not the baftard Heron²³ flain   39
   " Your warden,²⁴ with his fpiteful fpear ?
" The league and peace therefore are vain,
   " My liege, you nothing have to fear."
" Then manful Maxwell²⁵ answered sone,   40
   " My liege, the league is broke by right ;
" For th' Englifh King ought not to have gone
   " Againft your friend in France to fight.
" Have you in league not entred late   41
   " With Lewis,²⁶ chofen the French king ?
" And now you fee what great debate
   " Betwixt the king and him doth fpring.
" What greater kindnefs could you fhewe   42
   " Unto your friend, the king of France,
" Than in Englifh blood your blade imbrue,
   " Againft their land to lift your lance ?
" You know what hurt to you was done   43
   " By Englifh kings in times of old :
" Your borders burn'd, and Barwick²⁷ town
   " Still by ftrong hand they from you hold.
" Wherefore more time let's not confume   44
   " But fiercely fight that land againe."
" And then ftood up the proud lord Hume,²⁸
   " Of Scotland the chief chamberlaine.
" My liege," quoth he, " in all your life   45
   " More lucky fate could never fall ;
" For now that land with little grief
   " Unto your crown you conquer fhall.

" For England's king, you underftand,   46
   " To France is paft with all his peers ;
" There's none at home left in the land
   " But joult-head monks and burften freers.
" Or ragged rufticks without rules,   47
   " Or priefts prating for pudding fhives,
" Or millners madder than their mules,
   " Or wanton clerks waking their wives.
" There's not a lord left in England,   48
   " But all are gone beyond the fea,
" Both knight and baron with his band,
   " With ordinance or artillery."
The king then call'd to Dellamount[29]   49
   Which bodword out of France did bring ;
Quoth he, " the nobles' names pray note,
   " Who are encamp'd with th' Englifh king."
" That will I do, my liege," quoth he,   50
   " As many as I have at hert :
" First there's the great earl of Derbye
   " With one that's called lord Herbert.[30]
"There is anearl of antient race,   51
   " Plum'd up in proud and rich array ;
" His banner cafts a glittering grace,
   " A half-moon in a golden ray."
" That is the noble Piercy[31] plain,"   52
   The King did fay, and gave a ftamp,
" There is not fuch a lord again,
   " No, not in all King Henry's camp."

"There is a lord who bold doth bear   53
  "A talbot brave, a burly tyke,
"Whofe fathers ftruck France fo with fear
  "As made poor wives and children fkrike."
The king then anfwered at one word,   54
  "That is the earl of Shrewfburye."[33]
"There is likewife a lufty lord
  "Which called is the famed Darcye.[34]
"There's Dudley[35] and brave Dellaware[36]   55
  "And Druery,[37] great lords all three;
"The duke of Buckingham[38] is there,
  "Lord Cobham[39] and lord Willoughbye.[40]
"There is the earl of Effex[41] gay,   56
  "And Stafford ftout[42] earl of Wiltfhire;
"There is the earl of Kent, lord Gray,[43]
  "With haughty Haftings,[44] hot as fire.
"There is the marquefs Dorfet[45] brave,   57
  "Fitzwater[46] and Fitzleigh,[47] lords great;
"Of doughty knights the lufty lave
  "I never could by name repeat.
"There is a knight of the north countrye   58
  "Which leads a lufty plump of fpears;
"I know not what his name fhould be,
  "A boyft'rous bull all black he bears."
Lord Hume then anfwered, Loudon hight,[48] 59
  "This fame is Sir John Nevil[49] bold;
"King Henry hath not so hardy a knight
  "In all his camp, my coat I'll hold.

" He doth maintain, without all doubt,   60
    " The earl of Weftmoreland's eftate ;
" I know of old his ftomach ftout,
    " In England is not left his mate."
Then the king afk'd his lords all round   61
    If wars or peace they did prefer ?
They cry'd, and made the hall to found,
    " Let peace go back, and let's have war.
" Our armour is for ufage marr'd,   62
    " Both helmet, habergeon, and creft ;
" Our ftartling naggs, in ftable fpar'd,
    " Are waxen wild with too much reft.
" Our ftaves, that were both tall and ftraight 63
    " Wax crooked and are caft each where :
" Therefore in England let's go fight,
    " Our booties brave from them to bear."
The king rejoyced then to fee   64
    His lords fo lively hearts to have,
And to their words did foon agree,
    Complying to their pleafures brave.
To Lyon king at arms⁵⁰ he cry'd,   65
    And took to him a letter broad ;
Quoth he, " no longer look thou bide,
    " But towards France foon take thy road.
" To Terwin⁵¹ town take thou thy way,   66
    " And greet well there my brother-in-law,
" And bid him there no longer ftay,
    " But homeward to his country draw.

" And bid him ceafe his furious force   67
   " Againft my friend the king of France,
" For fear domeftick wars prove worfe
   " When in his kingdom I advance.
" And fummon him foon to return,   68
   " Left that our power we ply apace,
" With fire and fword we beat and burn
   " His men and land in little fpace."
Then Lyon made him reverence   69
   And with his coat of arms him deckt ;
He hal'd up fail, and towards France
   He did his way with fpeed direct.

THE SECOND FIT.

Meanwhile the king did letters write,   1
   Which fwifteft poft did nimbly bear
To all his lords which had delight
   With him in England arms to wear.
Then every lord and knight each where   2
   And barons bold in mufters met.
Each man made hafte to mend his gear,
   And fome their rufty pikes did whet.

Some made a mell of maffy lead   3
  Which iron all about did bind ;
Some made ftrong helmets for the head,
  And fome their grifly gifarings grind ;
Some made their battle-axes bright ;   4
  Some from their bills did rub the ruft ;
Some made long pikes and lances light,
  Some pikeforks for to join and thruft ;
Some did a fpear for weapon wield ;   5
  Some did their lufty geldings try ;
Some all with gold did gild their fhield,
  Some did with divers colours dye.
The plowmen hard their teams could take   6
  And to hard harnefs them convert,
Their fhares defenfive armour make,
  To fave the head and fhield the hert.
Dame Ceres did unfwerv'd remain,   7
  The fertile fields did lie untill'd ;
Outrageous Mars fo fore did reign
  That Scotland was with fury fill'd.
The king of Scots, then much inflam'd   8
  With joy to fee himfelf obey'd,
He did command his chamberlaine
  In England all the gang to lead.
The chamberlaine, lord Hume, in haft,   9
  Marchwarden he o'er eaft alfo—
Within the Englifh borders' breaft
  With full eight thoufand men did go,

And enter in Northumberland   10
   With banners bravely blaz'd and borne,
And finding none them to withſtand,
   Did ſtraight deſtroy both hay and corne.
They ſpoil'd and ravag'd all abroad.   11
   And on each ſide in booties brought :
The coarſer loons got geldings good,
   And droves of kine and cattle caught.
Moſt ſtately halls and buildings gay   12
   With ſacrilegious hands they burn ;—
And this has always been their way,
   Whenever they could ſerve their turn.
But happy Harrad[52] church i' the hill,   13
   Thou always 'ſcaped their barb'rous rage :
As thou wert once, ſo art thou ſtill,
   The wonder of the preſent age.
There judge Gaſcoigne,[53] once wiſely grave, 14
   With his fair dame entomb'd doth lye ;
And there lies Rudimond[54] so brave,
   In armour, by his familye ;
With other noble perſons too,   15
   For valour fam'd and piety :
Their monuments you now may view,
   Moſt ſweet and lovely to the eye.
But to return, for I digreſs :   16
   The Scots thus having over-run
The bordering parts and filled with preys,
   They thought to Scotland to return.

Sir William Bulmer being told   17
  Of this great rout and wild array,
Did ſtrait forecaſt all means he could
  The Scots in their return to ſlay.
Two hundred men himſelf did lead ;   18
  To him there came the borderers ſtout,
And divers gentlemen with ſpeed
  Repair'd to him with horſe and foot.
They were not all a thouſand men,   19
  But knowing where the Scots would come,
The borderers beſt their coaſts did ken,
  And hid them in a field of broom.
The Scots came ſcouring down ſo faſt,   20
  And proudly pricked up with their prey ;
Thinking their perils all were paſt,
  They ſtraggling ran out of their way.
The Engliſh men burſt out apace   21
  And ſkirmiſhed with the Scots anon :
There was fierce fighting face to face,
  And many geldings made to groan.
There men might ſee ſpears fly in ſpells   22
  And tall men tumbling on the ſoil ;
And many a horſe turn'd up his heels,—
  Outrageous Mars kept ſuch a coil.
The Scots their ſtrength did long extend,   23
  And broken ranks did ſtill renew ;
But the Engliſh archers, in the end,
  With arrows ſhot moſt ſore they ſlew.

The Englifh fpears, on the other fide,   24
  Amongft the Scots did fiercely fling,
Right through their ranks did rattling ride
  And chafe them thro' mofs, mire, and ling.
The chamberlaine, viewing this chance,   25
  And feeing his hoft all put to flight,
Did with the foremoft forth advance,
  But happy in his horfe fo light;
For ftraight he flew, when he perceiv'd   26
  His banner-bearer down was beat.
The Englifh then their fpoil receiv'd,
  Befides a ftore of geldings great.
Six hundred Scots were flain that day,   27
  And near that number prifoners ta'en;
But of the Englifh, brave and gay,
  There were no more than fixty flain.
In Auguft month this broil befell,   28
  Wherein the Scots loft fo much blood;
And mournful, when the tale they tell,
  They call it now The Devil's Road.
Thus while the Scots, both near and far,   29
  Were through all Scotland occupy'd
In framing weapons, fit for war,
  And muft'ring men on ev'ry fide;
By this time came the herald fent   30
  Before the town of Terwin high.
There to King Henry foon he went,
  And bow'd him low upon his knee,

Thus reverently the king did greet   31
  Who took from him his letters large,
And then, as order'd, what was writ
  In open words he did difcharge.
The letters soon were looked upon   32
  And in King Henry's fight peruf'd ;
King James' his mind he knew full foon,
  And found himfelf moft fore abuf'd,
Who fummon'd him his fiege to raife,   33
  And ftay thofe wars he took in hand ;
Or elfe with blood he'd pave his ways,
  And ftraight invade his native land.
King Henry's heart began to rife,   34
  And to the herald thus did fay,
" Thy mafter thus I did furmife
  " Would in our abfence partly play.
" Indeed he doth not now digrefs   35
  " From his old fires, never brave ;
" But if he do my land diftrefs,
  " I hope he welcome hard fhall have.
" For in my land I left a lord   36
  " Who, aiding of my royal queen,
" Will ftay your prince at point of fword,
  " Whofe blade was ever fierce and keen.
" Let him not deem fo deftitute   37
  " My land of lords and valiant knights ;
" For if he dare to profecute,
  " He there fhall find some warlike wights,

" Who'll fhed for me their purple gore,   38
    "And all his ftreaming banners rend ;
" They'll fend upon him many a fhower
    " Of arrows, e'er he pafs the Trent.

" For fince he perjur'd now doth prove,   39
    "And doth fo fmall efteem his oath,
" Our fiege we will not ceafe to move,
    " Be he fo never mad or wroth.

" But here a valiant vow we'll make :   40
    " At what time as we fhall return,
" All Scotland we will harafs and fack
    " And never ceafe to fpoil and burn,

" Nor never peace with him contrive,   41
    " Nor never league nor union make,
" While one falfe Scot is left alive,
    " And till the land be brought to wrack.

Then he to th' king of Scots did write   42
    A letter, banifhing all fears,
That he, for all his ire and fpite
    In France would ftill proceed his wars ;

Then gave it to the herald's hand,   43
    Befides with it a rich reward ;
Who haften'd to his native land,
    To fee how with his king it far'd,

But while he waited for the wind,   44
    And for his fhip did things ordain,
For all his hafte he came behind,
    And never faw his prince again.

King Henry then the Scottish bill   45
    Unto the earl of Surrey sent
To Pomfret, where abiding still
    He bid him be for battle bent.
The earl did all things straight provide   46
    The Scotch king's purpose to resist
Throughout all Scotland far and wide,
    And all was done that he did list.
Lord Dacres too, he did perceive   47
    The Scots' intention manifest ;
He knew their meetings, musters brave,
    And daily riding without rest.
The truth whereof he sent straitway,   48
    And told the earl of Surrey sage
That time was not for to delay,
    But soldiers raise for to engage.
Which when the earl did understand,   49
    He letters sent both far and near
To all the nobles in the land,
    That they their forces might prepare,
And tell what numbers they could make   50
    Of valiant men, all well array'd ;
Then with Sir Philip Tilney[54] spake,
    How they their wages might be paid.
Then after this for ordinance sent   51
    Unto Sir Nicholas Appleyard,[55]
Who did accordingly consent
    And towards him apace prepar'd.

With culverines and mortars[36] great, 52
   And double cannons two or three ;
He brought them on by ſtee and cart
   To Durham in the north countrye.
The noble lord then letters wrote 53
   Unto each caſtle, fort, and hold,
That they ſhould furniſh them with ſhot,
   And fortify their bulwarks bold,
Who anſwered all, with ſtomachs ſtout, 54
   And every captain with his train,
That they would keep the Scots quite out
   Until the king return'd again ;
Which anſwer of the captains keen 55
   The noble earl did much delight.
But what the Scots this while did mean,
   And of King James, I mean to write.
For after he to his brother-in-law 56
   Defiance into France had ſent,
His nobles all to him did draw,
   Well buſked and for battle bent.
And thus array'd in armour bright 57
   They met in Edinborough town :
There was many a lord, and many a knight
   And baron brave, of high renown.
Of prelates proud a populous lave, 58
   And abbots boldly there were known,
With biſhop of St. Andrew[37] brave,
   Who was King James's baſtard ſon.

Surelye t'was an unfeemly fight,   59
    And quite againft our Chriftian laws,
To fee a prelate prefs to fight,
    And that, too, in a wicked caufe.
Are thefe the Scots' religious rules   60
    Who taught the priefts fuch pranks perverfe :
To march forth muft'red on their mules,
    And, foldier-like, to fue god Mars ?
The meffenger of Chrift, St. Paul,   61
    Taught them to fhoot at no fuch mark ;
Peter, nor Chrift's apoftles all,
    They never led them in the dark.
Their patron fo did not them learn,   62
    St. Andrew,[58] with his fhored crofs ;
But rather Trimon of Quitorn,[59]
    Or Doffin,[60] demi-god of Rofs.
This bifhop bold, this baftard bleft,   63
    With other bifhops in his band,
And abbots bold as all the reft,
    For beagle rods took bills in hand.
And every lord with him did lead   64
    A mighty band for battel preft ;
In numbers great they did extend,
    A hundred thoufand men at leaft.
King James for joy began to fmile,   65
    So great an army to behold,
Who for to ferve him thought no toil,
    But blazen'd forth his banners bold.

Each lord went on then with his band,   66
  And every captain with his train;
The musick echo'd thro' the land,
  And brazen trumpets blow'd amain.
The drums did beat with warlick sound,   67
  And banners bravely waving wide;
Men scarce could view the fruitful ground
  But soldiers arm'd on every side.
In midst of ranks there rode the king   68
  On stately steed, which graceful stampt:
A goodly sight to see him sling,
  And how his foaming bits he champt.
Thus did King James most gorgeous ride,   69
  A pleasure to his noble peers;
He had a heart puffed up with pride,
  And was a prince that banish'd fears.
Alas! he thought himself too strong,   70
  Having so great a multitude;
But Providence, when kings do wrong,
  Their mighty power can elude.
He thought no king in Christendom   71
  In field to meet him was of might;
No, not an emperour of Rome
  Had been of force with him to fight.
Nor Hercules, nor Haniball,   72
  The Soldan, Sophy, nor the Turk,
None of the mighty monarchs all:
  Such valiant blood did in him work.

But yet for all his armed host,   73
   His puffed up pride and haughty heart,
Full foon abated was his ghoft,
   And brought to London in a cart.
'Twas in the midft of harveft tide,   74
   Auguft the two and twentieth day,
That this proud prince, replete with pride,
   To th' Englifh borders burft his way,
Where pills he pulled down apace,   75
   And ftately building brought to ground.
The Scots, like loons void of all grace,
   Religion's precepts fore did wound :
Fair matrons they did force each where,   76
   And ravish'd maidens fweet and mild,
In flames the houfes made appear,
   And murder'd many a man and child.
But how the Englifh did prepare   77
   To fight the Scots with hand and heart,
Their wit and valour will appear
   If you'll but read the second part.

The Famous History or Ballad

OF THE

BATTLES FOUGHT IN FLODDON FIELD,

Taken from an
Ancient Manuscript which was transcribed by
Mr. Richard Guy,
late Schoolmaster in Ingleton, Yorkshire.

Part II.

THE THIRD FIT.

(To a pleasant Tune.)

'Twas thus the king's express command,   1
  To waste with cruel sword and flame;
A field of blood he made the land,
  Till he to Norham[61] castle came,
Which soon with siege he did beset,   2
  And trenches digg'd without delay;
With bombard shot the walls he beat,
  And to assault it did essay.
The captain great with courage stout   3
  His fortress fiercely did defend;
But for a while he lashed out,
  Till he his ordinance did spend,

His powder did profufely wafte,   4
  His arrows hal'd out every hour,
So that he wanted at the laft,
  And at the laft had none to pour.
But yet five days he did defend,   5
  Tho' with affaults they him affail'd,
And all their total ftrength extend :
  But all their power had not prevail'd,
Was it not for a trait'rous thief   6
  Who came King James's face before,
That in that hold had got relief
  The fpace of thirty years and more.
"I fay," quoth he, "King James, my liege !   7
  "Your brave affaults are all in vain :
"Long may you hold a tedious fiege,
  "Yet all this while can get no gain.
"But what reward fhall I receive,"   8
  Quoth he, "exprefs and fpeak anon,
"And I fhall let you plain perceive
  "How that this caftle may be won ?"
"If that to pafs thou bring this can,"   9
  The king did fay where he did ftand,
"I fhall make you a gentleman,
  "And livings give thee in our land."
"O king !" quoth he, "then quit this place,   10
  "And down to yonder vallies draw :
"The walls fo fhall you rend and raze,
  "Your batteries will bring them low."

Which as he faid, fo did the king;   11
　　Againft the walls his ord'nance bent :
It was a wretched, difmal thing
　　To fee how foon the walls were rent ;
Which made the captain fore afraid,   12
　　Beholding how the walls they reel'd ;
His weapons all then down he laid,
　　And to King James did humbly yield.
The Scots then ftraitway did pour in,   13
　　And plied apace unto their prey :
Look what was worth one point or pin,
　　You need not bid them take away.
So when the Scots the walls had won,   14
　　And rifled every nook and place,
The traytor came to th' king anon,
　　But for reward met with difgrace.
The king then afk'd him by and by   15
　　Where he was born, and in what town ?
" A Scotsman, Sir !" he did reply,
　　Such anfwer gave the treacherous loon.
The king then afk'd him, meek and mild,   16
　　For how long he had lodged there ?
" Even," quoth he, " fince but a child,
　　" A good deal more than thirty year."
" Why," quo' the king, " haft thou fo wrought   17
　　" Unto thy friends this frantick rage,
" Who in this caftle thee upbrought,
　　" And always gave thee meat and wage ?

" But fince thy heart is falfify'd   18
  " To them who gave thee meat and fee,
" It is a token to be try'd,
  " Thou never canft prove true to me.
" Therefore for this thy traiterous trick   19
  " Thou fhalt be tyed in a trace !
" Hangman, therefore," quoth he, " be quick,
  " The groom fhall have no better place."
What he did fay, forthwith was wrought ;   20
  The traytor had his juft defert,
Although the king himfelf was naught,
  And prov'd deceitful in his hert.
By this time came the flying pofts,   21
  Which made the earl to underftand
How that the king of Scotland's hofts
  Already ent'red had the land ;
Which when the earl of Surrey knew,   22
  It was but vain to bid him hafte :
He fent to all his friends moft true,
  That they their men fhould mufter faft ;
And fhortly fent to every fhire,   23
  That on September the firft day,
Each gentleman, lord, knight, and fquire,
  Should to Newcaftle take their way.
Then with five hundred foldiers ftout   24
  Himfelf appearing in renown,
He never ftay'd to reft his foot,
  Until he came to Durham town.

There he devoutly did hear prayers,
　　And worſhip'd God his Maker dear,
Who baniſh'd from him cares and fears :
　　St. Cuthbert's[62] banner he did bear.
Then ſtrait he to Newcaſtle came,　　　26
　　Of Auguſt on the thirtieth day,
There many a nobleman of fame
　　To him repair'd without delay.
The valiant Dacres[3] him did meet,　　　27
　　And brought with him a noble band
Of warlike men right well compleat,
　　From Weſtmoreland and Cumberland.
Sir Marmaduke Conſtable[63] ſtout　　　28
　　Attended with his lovely ſons ;
Sir William Bulmer,[15] with his rout ;
　　Lord Clifford[11] with his clapping guns.
Then from Newcaſtle ſoon he went,　　　29
　　And took his way to Anwick town,
That weary men, with travel ſpent,
　　And weather-beaten, might have roon.
Then might you ſee on every ſide　　　30
　　The ways all fill'd with men of war,
With ſhining ſtreamers waving wide,
　　And helmets glittering from afar.
From Lancaſhire and Cheſhire too,　　　31
　　To Stanley came a noble train
To Hornby, from whence he withdrew,
　　And forward ſet with all his main.

What banners brave before him blaz'd   32
   The people muf'd where he did pafs ;
Poor hufbandmen were much amaz'd,
   And women, wond'ring, cry'd " Alas !"
Young wives did weep with woful chear,   33
   To fee their friends in harnefs dreft ;
Some rent their cloaths, fome tore their hair,
   Some held their babes unto their breaft.
And woful mothers mourning ftood,   34
   Viewing their fons in harnefs horfe,
And fhouting fhrieked when forth they rode,
   And of their lives took little force.[64]
But who can plain exprefs with pen,   35
   What maffes[65] faid on hallow'd ftone,
What prayers of religious men,
   What facred fervice eke was done,
That Stanley might come fafe away,   36
   And victor valiantly return.
The bells did found a-night and day,
   And holy fires bright did burn.
Men with grey beards drew to their beds,   37
   And faft their prayers they poured out ;
Old wives for woe did wag their heads,
   And faints were fought on naked foot.
But Stanley over Stainmore[66] ftrait   38
   Did pafs, and refting there did view
A banner brave borne up on hight,
   Whereunder went a warlike crew.

" What lufty troop in yon I fee ?"   39
   Sir Edward Stanley did enquire.
A yeoman faid, " It is, I fee,
   " Bryan Tunftall[67] that bold efquire ;
" For in his banner I behold   40
   " A curling cock, as tho' he'd crow ;
" He brings with him his tenants bold,
   " A hundred men at leaft, I know."
Then Stanley faid, as there he ftood,   41
   " Would Chrift he would but take our part,
" His clean and undefiled blood
   " Good fpeed doth promife at my heart.
" Blaze out, therefore, I bid you, foon   42
   " The earl of Darby's banner brave ;
" By chance with us he will be one
   " When it in fight he fhall perceive."
But Tunftall took no heed that tide ;   43
   Without faluting forth he paft :
Upon the valiant Howard's fide
   His faithful heart he fixed faft.
And then again faid Stanley brave,   44
   " O valiant lads, draw up your hearts !
" Be not amaz'd, look not fo grave,
   " Tho' Tunftall will not take our parts,
" But forward fet without delay ;   45
   " Unto the Howard's let's make haft."
And fo they wearied kept their way,
   Till they to Anwick came at laft ;

Whofe coming greatly did rejoice   46
   The earl and all his companye.
None but the eagle bare the voice,
   With flapping wings as he would fly.
There did the army much increafe,   47
   Although there was the moft extreams ;
For rain down rattling ne'er did ceafe,
   Till bubbling brooks burft mighty ftreams.
Such bluft'ring winds befides there were,   48
   That day and night the air did found ;
Which put the earl into great fear
   Left his fon admiral²¹ fhould be drown'd,
Who, at his parting, promif'd plight   49
   Unto his father, if alive,
At Newcaftle with all his might
   For his affiftance fhould arrive.
Which promife he did fully keep ;   50
   Such kindly friendfhip Neptune fhow'd,
As to conduct him o'er the deep,
   And his defires juft beftow'd.
Then foldiers foon he fet on land,   51
   And to his father faft he hy'd ;
Such warlike wights in worthy band,
   Two thoufand men in arms well try'd,
With captains moft courageous keen,   52
   At Anwick they arriv'd at laft,
Who when the earl's army they had feen,
   With fudden fear they were aghaft.

Seeing their armour black as ink,   53
    Some faid it was fome Scottifh band ;
And divers did efteem and think
    They were fome force from foreign land.
Some took their harnefs, fome their horfe   54
    And forward hafted as to fight ;
But when they faw St. George's crofs
    And Englifh arms borne up on hight,
Some faid it was a jolly crew   55
    The king had fent from France that tide.
The fouthern men the truth foon knew,
    And loud " Lord Admiral " they cry'd.
Who when the earl of Surrey faw,   56
    He thanked God with hert fo mild,
And hands for joy to heaven did throw,
    His fon was fav'd from waters wild.
A merry meeting there was feen,   57
    For firft they kift, and then embrac'd ;
For joy the tears fell from their eyen ;
    All forepaft fears were then defac'd.
Then cauf'd the earl each captain count   58
    Under their wings what foldiers were ;
Which done, the number did but mount
    To fix and twenty thoufand there.
The earl then called a council fone   59
    Of prudent lords and captains wife,
And how the battle might be done,
    He bid them fhew their beft device.

Some faid too fmall their number was   60
  To atchieve fo great an enterprize ;
Some councell'd pofts back for to pafs
  For aid, and caufe the counties rife ;
And from the fouth the queen, fome faid,   61
  A band of foldiers foon would fend ;
And will'd to ftay, for while they ftay'd,
  Their powers daily might amend.
Some faid the Scots ftraitway would fail,   62
  And powers daily would diminifh ;
Wherefore to ftay was their counfeil,
  And thus the earl they did admonifh.
Then did the admiral ftart in ire,   63
  And ftamping ftood with ftomach hot ;
" Why, Sir !" faid he there to his fire,
  " Hath cowardice lent you his coat ?
" Let ne'er King Henry hear for fhame   64
  " That you fhould play this daftard part ;
" Nor ever blown by trump of fame
  " That you did bear a coward's heart !
" Hath not King Henry left you here   65
  " His governour, to rule the land ?
" Not doubting but without all feare,
  " The treacherous Scots you would withftand.
" Think of your father,[6s] tho' his chance   66
  " It was to fall at Bofworth feild,
" Tho' he his life, by Stanley's lance,
  " With honourable wounds did yeild.

" Would God that Edward,[19] brother dear,   67
  " Was here alive this prefent day :
" No armed foes could make him fear,
  " Nor in a camp, like coward, ftay.
" What royal fame, what high renown,   68
  " Hath he left to his line and race !
" What ample glory would him crown,
  " If life had lafted longer fpace
" The feas he did both fweep and fcour,   69
  " No pyrate proud durft 'pear in fight,
" Not pyrate John,[22] for all his power,
  " That great renowned Lothian knight.
" How oft the royal fleet of France   70
  " In conflicts cruel by him was griev'd !
" If he had 'fcaped that fatal chance,
  " What glorious acts might have atchiev'd !
" No multitudes made him difmay'd ;   71
  " Nor numbers great his ftomach 'fwage.
" Great fhame would then on us be laid,
  " And to our offspring in each age ;
" Your father's fame would foon be loft,   72
  " And all his worthy acts no more ;
" Your honour, like a flitting ghoft.
  " Nor yet your fons could e'er reftore :
" If here ye loit'ring lie like loons,   73
  " And do not fight the Scots again :
" For don't you hear how Englifh towns
  " Are burnt, and fuckling babes are flain ?

" They daily pilfer every place   74
    " And fpoil the people all about :
" Wherefore let's ftay no longer fpace,
    " But now ftep forth with ftomachs ftout."

THE FOURTH FIT.

The Earl of Surrey then reply'd   1
    And to his warlike fon did fay,
" No bafhfulnefs doth make me 'bide,
    " Nor ftomach faint doth make me ftay.
" The caufe is for no cowardice,   2
    " So long time here to make delay ;
" But that I fear this enterprize
    " Will prove no childifh fport or play.
" Great counfel then muft be embrac'd ;   3
    " Then let us careful think upon,
" Which way our cards to count and caft,
    " For great's the bufinefs to be done.
" Too hardy oft good hap doth hazard,   4
    " And over-bold oft is not beft ;
" And that I've prov'd by my fon Edward.[69]
    " Who ever was too bold off Breft.

" He'd been a living man this day,   5
    " If he with counfel wife had wrought ;
" But he was drown'd in Bartrumb's[70] bay :
    " His rafhnefs to this end him brought.
" My father, at king Richard's feild,[71]   6
    " Under great Stanley's[72] lance lay flain,
" And I did there a captive yeild :
    " Our manhood great got us this gain.
" We might have 'fcap'd that fcurvy day,   7
    " If warning could our wits have bet :
" A friend of ours, to caufe us ftay,
    " Upon my father's gate had fet
" A certain fcroll, whofe fcripture faid :—   8
    " Jack of Norfolk, be not too bold !
" And underneath in verfe was laid :—
    " Dickon thy mafter's bought and fold !
" My father fighting fierce was flain,   9
    " King Richard 'reaved of life and crown :
" Such goodly guerdon oft they gain,
    " Who rafhly run to get renown.
" For fee the duke of York was brought   10
    " At Wakefield to his fatal fall,
" Who might have 'fcap'd, if he had wrought
    " The counfel wife of David Hall.[73]
" I read of conquerors and kings   11
    " For lack of counfel caft away :
" Now fince at hand fuch danger hings,
    " Our counfel we had need to fay.

" It is not I am fright with fear,   12
    " Nor for myfelf fuch thought I take,
" But for young babes and infants dear,
    "Which fathers, fore I fear, will lack.
" Such fortunes fall thro' fights doubtlefs,   13
    " Poor widows plenty fhall be left,
" And many a fervant mafterlefs,
    " And mothers of their fons bereft.·
" This is the caufe I counfel crave,   14
    " The only caufe I caft fuch doubts ;
" I'd rather one Englifh foldier fave
    " Than for to kill a thoufand Scots.
" I can no kind of compafs caft,   15
    " But many a life there muft be loft,
" And many a tall man death muft taft,
    " The Scots are fuch a mighty hoft.
" The prince himfelf is there prefent   16
    " With all his peers, prepar'd for war,
" With barons, knights, and commons bent,
    " A hundred thoufand men they are
" Put cafe, our total Englifh power   17
    " Were ready dreft and made in meat :
" At two meals they would us devour,
    " The Scottifh army is fo great.
" Therefore let each man's mind b'expreft   18
    " How that the Scots we may convince,
" And how to pafs this peril beft,
    " And fave the honour of our prince."

Then fpake Sir Edward Stanley ftout,   19
   And fierce on th'earl he fixt his eyen,
" What need have we thus for to doubt,
   " And be afraid of foes unfeen ?
" Shall we, by loit'ring on this manner,   20
   " Thus ftill permit the Scots to reft ?
" Fye! let them fee an Englifh banner,
   " And view our foldiers feemly dreft.
" What though our foes be five to one,   21
   " For that let not our ftomachs fail :
" God gives the ftroke when all is done,
   " If it pleafe him, we fhall prevail.
" If antient records we perufe,   22
   " Set forth by famous clerks of old,
" Which both of Chriftians, Pagans, Jews,
   " Do plain defcribe the battles bold :
" There may we certain fee in fight   23
   " Many a mighty prince and king,
" With populous armies, put to flight
   " And vanquifh'd by a little wing.
" With hundreds three, Judge Gideon   24
   " The Midian hoft o'ercame in fight ;
" And Jonathan, Saul's valiant fon,
   " The fierce Philiftines put to flight.
" So Judas Machabees, the man   25
   " Of foremoft fame among all knights,
" Who can defcribe what feilds he wan
   " With handfulls fmall of warlike wights ?

" The mighty Macedonian prince,   26
    " With puiffance fmall and power,
" King Darius' hoft did all convince,
    " Who were for one in number four.
" The great renowned Roman peers,   27
    " Whofe glorious praife can never blin
" Nor fame that daily fills men's ears,
    " Through numbers great did never win.
" But Titus Livy doth proteft,   28
    " The lefs their power, the more their gain ;
" When they were moft they wan the leaft,
    " The greater prefs, more people flain.
" Example : at Cannæ's fierce conflict   29
    " So many nobles there were flain,
" That bufhels three they did collect
    " Of rings from dead men's fingers ta'en.
" Where Scipio, with numbers fmall   30
    " Of warlike wights of lufty blood,
" In feild to flight put Haniball,
    " And burnt with fire Carthage proud.
" What further need I for to feek   31
    " Of Chriftian kings their manful acts,
" Since records of the fame ftill fpeak,
    " Of Henry and his famous facts.
" All Europe yet afrefh doth found   32
    " Of his high prowefs's report.
" What ftandards ftout brought he to ground
    " With numbers fmall at Agincourt !

" All France yet trembleth to hear talk,   33
  " What nobles unto death were dight :
" Two thoufand, befides vulgar folk,
  " Simpleft of whom was fquire or knight.
" He never ftint from war and ftrife   34
  " Till th'heir of France he was proclaim'd.
" If fate had lent him longer life,
  " With Englifh laws all France he'd fram'd.
" Of Bedford eke his brother John,[74]   35
  " The dolphin bet with a fmall band ;
" Lord Talbot[75] with his name alone
  " To tremble forc'd all the French land.
" The earl of Richmond, with fmall power,   36
  " Of England wan both realm and crown
" At Bofworth, where the raging boar[76]
  " And all his hoft were overthrown.
" So though the Scottifh hoft be great,   37
  " Let us not ftint, but them withftand ;
" In battle bold we fhall them beat,
  " For God will help us with His hand.
" But if in fighting we are flain   38
  " And be in battle brought to ground,
" Perpetual praife we then fhall gain,
  " Men will our fame for aye out-found.
" The mem'ry of our great manhood   39
  " 'Mongft Englifhmen for aye fhall laft ;
" And then for vengeance of our blood
  " King Henry home from France will haft.

" Our kinsfolk and our coufins free   40
 " Will wreak our deaths with doleful dint ;
" Till time that they revenged be,
 " From fturdy ftrokes they will not ftint.
" Our ghofts fhall go to God on high,   41
 " Though bodies vile to death be dight ;
" In better cafe we cannot die,
 " Than fighting for our country's right.
" Put cafe, the lot light contrary,   42
 " As firm my faith is fixt it fhall,
" And that to gain the victory
 " Good fortune on our fide fhall fall ;
" And that we give our foes the foil,   43
 " What worthy praifes fhall we win !
" What mighty prey ! what plenteous fpoil !
 " What prifoners of princely kin !
" The prince is there himfelf, King Jame,   44
 " With prelates paffing rich in pride ;
" Fifty great lords there are of fame,
 " With barons, knights, and fquires befide ;
" Whofe tents, if ftanding they be found   45
 " When fight is done, I do not fear.
" But for their ent'ring Englifh ground
 " Their charges they fhall pay full dear.
" Such fate fhall fall to them, I truft,   46
 " As to their elders has before
" Who dar'd into our borders bruft,
 " When they were beat in battle fore.

"Their mighty Mars, King Malchomye,[77]   47
  "Did valiantly this land invade ;
"At Tinmoth he was forc'd to flee,
  "And flain was by an Englifh blade.
"King David[78] unto Durham came,   48
  "Who with the Scots in pitched feild,
"For all their pride, yet loft the game ;
  "King David there did captive yeild.
"What fhall I further mention mack   49
  "Of Henry Fourth, how in his days
"Th' earl of Morray and lords Mordack,
  "Angus, and Douglafs,[79] prickt with praife,
"Did enter in Northumberland   50
  "And murthered men without mercye.
"Were they not bet by a fmall band
  "In battle, by Sir Henry Piercye ?
"The ftory faith, who lift to looke,   51
  "Ten thoufand Scots in field were flaine,
"And through the valiant Piercy's ftroke
  "All the earls captives did remaine.
"Such luck, I truft, to our foes will light   52
  "And all that wars do raife in wrong ;
"Wherefore againft them let us fight,
  "It's fhame we loiter here fo long.
"If any feem abaf'd to be   53
  "That we in battle fhall be bet,
"Chefhire and Lancafhire with me
  "Shall give the Scots the firft onfet."

When this was faid, then Stanley ftout   54
   All filent down did fit in place ;
The eyen of all the lords about
   Were fixed on his valiant face.
His wifdom great all wonder'd at,   55
   And all his manful proffer praif'd ;
All they that would have ling'red lat,
   Their courage great was now upraif'd.
Now they that lately would have ftay'd,   56
   With foremoft cry'd " Forth to the feild !"
With one voice all the earl they pray'd
   That Stanley might the vanguard weild.
But on that fide the earl of Surrey   57
   Was deaf ; for why, he would not hear.
For being mov'd with Stanley's glory,
   His rancour old then did appear.
Quoth he, " The king's place I fupply ;   58
   " At pleafure mine each thing fhall 'bide."
Then on each captain he did cry
   In prefence to appear that tide.
That done, ftraitway he did ordain   59
   His battle brief on this fame fort,
Whofe order and array right plain
   With pen I fhall make true report.

The Famous History or Ballad

OF THE

BATTLES FOUGHT IN FLODDON FIELD,

Taken from an
Ancient Manuscript which was transcribed by
Mr. Richard Guy,
late Schoolmaster in Ingleton, Yorkshire.

Part III.

THE FIFTH FIT.

(To a pleasant Tune.)

Now when Stanley with ftomach ftout   1
  Did valiantly the vanguard crave,
The earl of Surrey fore did doubt,
  That too high honour he fhould have.
If fortune good fell on his part   2
  And valiant victor he'd return.
'Gainft Stanley's blood fuch hateful heart
  In the earl's breaft did boiling burn.
Wherefore in forward, firft of all,   3
  Chief captain conftituted he
His loving fon, lord admirall,
With foldiers fuch as came from fea.

Whom valiant lords accompany'd,   4
 With barons bold, and hardy knights ;
Lord Ogle[60] one, of courage try'd,
 Who led a band of warlike wights.
In order, next the admirall,   5
 The lufty knight lord Clifford[11] went,
Who was conceal'd in fhepherd's caul,
 Till twice twelve years were gone and fpent.
For when his father at Wakefield   6
 The duke of York' his fon had flaine,
He by a friend was thus conceal'd
 Till Richmond's earl began his raigne,
Who him reftor'd to all his right,   7
 Seating him in his fire's land ;
Or elfe to death he had been dight,
 While th' houfe of York had the uphand.
Now like a captain bold he brought   8
 A band of lufty lads elect,
Whofe curious coats, moft cunning wrought,
 With dreadful dragons were bedeckt :
From Penigent to Pendlehill,   9
 From Linton to Long Addingham,
And all that Craven coafts did till,
 They with the lufty Clifford came.
All Staincliff hundred went with him,   10
 With ftriplings ftrong from Worledale,
And all that Hauton[51] hills did climb,
 With Langftroth eke and Littondale,

Whofe milkfed fellows, flefhly bred.   11
  Well brawn'd, their founding bows upbend ;
All fuch as Horton fells had fed,
  On Clifford's banner did attend.
Next whom lord Lumley and Latimer[81]   12
  Were equal matcht with all their power,
With whom was next their neighbour near,
  Lord Coniers[83] ftout and ftiff in ftour,
With many a gentleman and fquire   13
  From Rippon, Ripley. and Ryedale.
With them marcht forth all Maffamfhire,
  With Noifterfield and Netherdale,
With tillmen tough in harnefs ftore,   14
  Which turn'd the furrows of Mitton feild,
With billmen bold from Blackamoor :[84]
  Moft warlike wights thefe lords did weild.
Next whom was plac'd with all his power   15
  Lord Scroop[13] of Upfall, th' aged knight ;
Sir Stephen Bull,[85] fo ftiff in ftour,
  Was matcht next him with all his might.
Sir Walter Aufith,[86] fage and grave,   16
  Was with Sir Henry Sherburn[87] bent,
And under Bulmer's banner brave
  Th' whole bifhoprick of Durham went ;
Whom enfued Sir Chriftopher Ward,[88]   17
  With him Sir Edward Effingham ;
Next went Sir Nicholas Appleyard,
  Sir Metham Sidney Everingham :

All thefe in foremoft battle bold,   18
    These valiant wights in vanguard were :
Seven thoufand men numb'red and told,
    Simpleft of whom bare bow or fpear.
Then the earl Sir Edmond Howard   19
    'Gan call, whom marfhall foon he made ;
" My fon," faid he, " now foon fet forth,
    " With valiant heart the Scots invade.
" Chief captain of the right hand wing   20
    " To brother thine I thee ordain.
" Full furely fee thou ferve the king,
    " Employ thy power, let for no pain ;
" Of fouthern foldiers hundreds two   21
    " Under thy wing fhall wend with thee."
A thoufand thanks Sir Edmund too
    Did render to his father free.
With him was matcht as equal mate   22
    Bryan Tunftall,[67] that trufty fquire,
Whofe ftomach ftout nought could abate
    Nor ought could fwage his bold defire.
The glory of his grandfire old,   23
    The famous acts eke of his fire,
His blood untainted made him bold
    And ftirr'd his ftomach hot as fire.
For when debate did firft begin,   24
    And rancour raifed moft rueful work
And ruffling rul'd this realm within,
    'Twixt Lancafter and th' houfe of York ;

During which hurly-burly and ftrife   25
   Were murther'd many a mother's child,
And many a lord bereav'd of life,
   And noble houfe with blood defil'd,—
Yet this man's father, void of feare,   26
   While in this realm fuch ruffling was,
To Henry Sixth did ftill adhere
   And for no pains would from him pafs.
For he to York would never yeild   27
   For all the ftruggling, ftir, and ftrife ;
Nine times he fiercely fought in feild,
   So oft in danger was his life.
And when the king was captive caught   28
   And th' earl of Warwick overthrown,
To fave his life beft means he fought.
   And was in bark to Britain blown.
With th' earl of Richmond he remain'd   29
   And lords of the Lancaftrian kin.
When th' earl at length the garland gain'd,
   And did fair England's empire win,
He render'd Tunftall all his right,   30
   And knowing his pure blood unblam'd,
He eke did caufe the trufty knight
   Undefil'd Tunftall to be nam'd.
Moft fierce he fought at th' fallow feild,   31
   Where Martin Swart[89] on ground lay flain.
When rage did reign, he never reel'd,
   But like a rock did ftill remain.

Now came this man, amongst the rest,   32
  To match his father in manhood,
For battle ready bent and prest,
  With him a band of lusty blood.
Next went Sir Bold[90] and Butler[91] brave,   33
  Two lusty knights of Lancashire ;
Then Barkeston bold, and Bygot grave,
  With Warcop wild, a worthy squire ;
Next Richard Chomley,[92] and Chifton stout, 34
  With men of Hatfield and of Hull ;
Lawrence of Dun, with all his rout,
  The people fresh with them did pull.
John Clartice then was 'nexed near ;   35
  With Stapylton of stomach stern ;
Next whom Fitzwilliam forth did fare
  Who martial feats was not to learn.
These captains keen with all their might   36
  In right-hand wing did warlike wend ;
All these on Edward Howard, knight,
  The earl, his sire, ordain'd to attend.
Then next the left-hand wing did weild   37
  Sir Marmaduke Constable[63] old ;
With him a troop well tried in feild,
  And eke his sons and kinsfolk bold.
Next him Sir William Piercy[32] proud   38
  Went with the great earl Piercy's power,
From Lancashire of lusty blood,
  A thousand soldiers, stiff in stowre.

The earl himſelf did undertake   39
   Of the rearward the regiment,
Whom barons bold did bravely back,
   And ſouthern ſoldiers ſeemly bent.
Next whom in place was 'nexed near   40
   Lord Scroop[93] of Bolton ſtern and ſtout,
On horſeback who had not his peer ;
   No Engliſhman Scots did more doubt.
With him did wend all Wenſledale   41
   From Morton unto Moiſdale moor ;
All they that dwelt by the banks of Swale,
   With him were bent in harneſs ſtour.
From Wenſdale warlike wights did wend ;   42
   From Biſhopſdale went bowmen bold,
From Coverdale to Cotter End,
   And all to Kidſon Cauſey cold ;[94]
From Mollerſtang and Middleham,   43
   And all from Marſk and Middletonby,
And all that climb the mountain Cam
   Whoſe crown from froſt is ſeldom free ;
With luſty lads and large of length,   44
   Which dwelt at Seimer water ſide ;
All Richmondſhire its total ſtrength
   The luſty Scroop did lead and guide.
Next went Sir Philip Tilney tall,   45
   With him Sir Thomas Barkley brave ;
Sir John Radcliffe in arms royall,
   And eke Sir William Gaſcoyn grave.[95]

Next whom did pafs with all his rout   46
  Sir Chriftopher Pickering proud,
Sir Bryan Stapylton moft ftout,
  Two valiant knights of noble blood.[96]
Next with Sir John Stanley there yede   47
  The bifhop of Ely's fervants bold ;
Sir Lionel Piercy,[32] eke did lead
  Some hundred men well tried and told.
Next went Sir Ninian Markenfil[97]   48
  In armour coat of cunning work ;
The next went Sir John Maundevill,[98]
  With him the citizens of York.
Sir George Darcy[34] in banner bright   49
  Did bear a bloody broken fpear ;
Next went Sir Magnus with his might,
  And Cheftane bold of lufty chear ;
Sir Guy Dawnie[99] with his glorious rout.   50
  Then Mr. Dawbie's fervants bold ;
Then Richard Tempeft[100] with his rout
  In rereward thus th' array did hold :
The right hand wing with all his rout   51
  The lufty lord Dacres[8] did lead ;
With him the bows of Kendal ftout
  With milkwhite coats and croffes red ;
All Kefwick eke and Cockermouth   52
  And all from Copeland's craggy hills ;
All Weftmoreland, both north and fouth,
  Whofe weapons were great weighty bills :

All Carlifle eke and Cumberland,   53
   They with lord Dacres proud did pafs,
From Branton and from Broughly fands,
   From Grayfton and from Ravenglafs,
With ftriplings ftrong from Stanemore fide ; 54
   And Auston-moor men marched even ;
All thofe that Gilfland grave did hide,
   With horfemen light from Hexham Leven :
All thefe did march in Dacres' band,   55
   All thefe enfu'd his banner broad ;
No luftier lord was in the land,
   Nor more might boaft of birth and blood.
Many ftrong houfes, huge of height,   56
   Were all his own to give or fell,
Fair baronies by his birth-right
   And heritage to him befell.
Thefe royal lords thus 'ray did hold,   57
   With ranges, ranks, and warlike wings ;
But yet the man is left untold
   On whom the matter wholly hings,
Whofe worthy praife and prowefs great,   58
   Whofe glorious fame fhall never blin,
Nor Neptune never fhall forget
   What laud he hath left to his kin.
Sir Edward Stanley, ftiff in ftour,   59
   He is the man of whom I mean ;
With him did pafs a mighty power
   Of foldiers feemly to be feen.

Moſt liver lads in Lonſdale bred,   60
  With weapons of unweildy weight ;
All ſuch as Tatham fells had fed
  Went under Stanley's ſtreamer bright.
From Bolland billmen bold were boun,   61
  With ſuch as Botton Banks did hide ;
From Wharmore up to Whittington,
  And all to Wenning water-ſide ;
From Silverdale to Kent Sand ſide   62
  Whoſe ſoil is ſown with cockle ſhells,
From Cartmell eke and Conneyſide,
  With fellows fierce from Furneſs fells ;
All Lancaſhire, for the moſt part,   63
  The luſty Stanley ſtout did lead,
A ſtock of ſtriplings ſtrong of heart,
  Brought up from babes with beef and bread ;
From Warton unto Warrington,   64
  From Wigan unto Wireſdale,
From Wedicar to Waddington
  From old Ribcheſter to Ratchdale ;
From Poulton and Preſton, with pikes   65
  They with the Stanley ſtout forth went ;
From Pemberton and Pilling dikes
  For battle billmen bold were bent ;
With fellows freſh and fierce in fight   66
  Which Horton fields turn'd out in ſcores,
With luſty lads, liver and light,
  From Blackburn and Bolton-i'th'moors ;

With children chofen from Chefhire,   67
  In armour bold for battle dreft,
And many a gentleman and fquire
  Were under Stanley's ftreamer preft.
Thus Stanley ftout, the laft of all,   68
  Of the rereward the rule did weild,
Which done, to Bolton in Glendale
  The total army took the feild,
Where all the counfel did confent   69
  That Rouge-Croix to the Scottifh king
Strait with inftructions fhould be fent
  To know his majefty's meaning.

THE SIXTH FIT.

And whereas the caftle of Ford   1
  He threat'ned for to overthrow,
Rouge-Croix was charged, word for word
  The earl's intent to let him know:—
That if the king would fo agree   2
  To fuffer that fame fort to ftand,
And William Heron[24] fend home free,
  Who then was captive in Scotland,

Whereto if th' king would condescend,   3
   The earl promifed to reftore
And to the king ftraitway to fend
   Of his countrymen captives four,
Lord Johnftone and Sir Sandy Hume,   4
   Sir Richard Hume and William Carr.[101]
But if the king fhould yet prefume
   In wrongful fort to raife up war
Againft King Henry, his brother-in-law,   5
   And commons cruelly did kill,
And pills and forts did fierce down draw,
   And Englifh blood fpar'd not fpill :
The earl charged the herald ftraight   6
   To certify the faid Scots' king,
That he in feild with him would fight
   On Friday then next following.
And then ere Rouge-Croix forth did fare,   7
   The admiral took him afide,
And bad him to the king declare
   His coming and accefs that tide ;
That he from fea defcended was   8
   With all his total power and might,
And that in forward with his grace
   He fhould him find fit for to fight ;
And when the Scots on him did call   9
   At days of March to make redrefs
For Andrew Barton, their admirall,
   Whom he with bloody blade did blefs,—

Now he was come in perfon preft   10
   The faid Sir Andrew's death to 'vouch ;
"And if it in his power doth reft,"
   Quoth he, " I fhall ferve him with fuch.
" For there fhall no Scot 'fcape unflain,   11
   " The king in perfon fole except ;
" For fo of th' Scots," quoth he again,
   " No other mercy I expect."
And yet ere Rouge-Croix went his way,   12
   The earl and counfel did expect
That the Scots king without delay
   An herald would again direct.
Rouge-Croix was yet commanded there   13
   No Scotsman near the field to bring,
Left he their conduct might declare,
   And thereby dangers great might fpring.
Then Rouge-Croix ready took his horfe,   14
   Bedeckt with coat of arms moft brave ;
With him did wend a trumpet hoarfe,
   That Scots their coming might perceive.
Their geldings were both good and light,   15
   From galloping they feldom ftay'd,
Till at the length they view'd in fight
   Where as their enemy's army laid.
The Scots watch them anon defcry'd   16
   And them convey'd before the king,
Where he with barons bold did 'bide,
   Whom Rouge-Croix on knees kneeling

With feemly falutations greet,   17
   And after, his inftructions ftraight
Each one expreft in order meet,
   And letters 'livered there in fight.
Whom when the king of Scots had heard,   18
   And eke had view'd his letters large,
E'en frantick-like he fuming far'd
   And, bombard-like, did boafts difcharge.
" If true," quoth he, " let't be expreft ;   19
   " Thou herald fent, anon recite !
"And was your earl fo bold of breaft
   " Thus proudly to a prince to write ?
'· But fince he feems to be fo rough,   20
   " I fwear," quoth he, " by fceptre and crown,
" He fhall have fighting fill enough
   " On Friday, fore the sun go down.
" For here to God I promife plight :   21
   " We never part will from this hill
" Till we have try'd your earl's whole might
   " And gi'en their folks fighting their fill.
" Becaufe he vex'd our land of late,   22
   " Perchance his ftomach is extoll'd ;
" But now we will withftand his grace
   " Or thoufand pates fhall there be poll'd."
To prefence then he call'd his peers,   23
   To whom he read the earl his bill,
And, audience given with ireful ears,
   Some faid it came of little fkill,

An earl of fo fimple a fhire   24
  To 'nointed king fuch words to write ;
Some bad the fchedule caft in fire ;
  Some for to fpeak did fpare for fpite ;
Some faid the herald of's own head   25
  Such talk extempore did exprefs,
And counfelled to ufe all fpeed
  An herald hafty to addrefs,
To know of th' earl of Surrey plain,   26
  If he fuch meffage did procure ;
And till the time he turn'd again
  The Englifh herald to make fure.
Whereto the king did foon confent,   27
  And Rougecroix fure in fafety kept ;
And home with th' Englifh trumpet fent
  An herald by name Ilay clept,
Who was commanded for to know   28
  Of the earl and his council fage
If Rougecroix truth to him did fhow,
  Or, if he had fent fuch meffage.
And if true tidings he had brought,   29
  And to his grace avouch'd no lye,
The king anon in mind forethought
  How he the earl might certifye.
He Ilay then inftructed ftraight   30
  With letters large and eloquent ;
Which done they foon fet forth that night
  And t'ards the Englifh camp they went.

But at a little village poor   31
    Ilay did light and took lodging ;
For th' army was two miles or more,
    Whiles trumpet fhews of his coming.
The night was even at midft well near,   32
    And th' Englifh lords lying on grafs ;
Till time the trumpet did appear
    And told earl Surrey all the cafe ;
How that the Scots they did detain   33
    Rougecroix, and credit him would not,
And for to know the truth more plain
    The king himfelf had fent a Scot,
Which he conftrained for to ftay   34
    And lodged in a village mean,
Left he their order might difplay,
    And fo the Scots advantage gain.
Which when the earl had underftood,   35
    And view'd the Scotchmen's dealings all
He in a found and fober mood
    Upon his council ftraight did call,
Where he in prefence did repeat   36
    The total tale the trumpet told.
The council muf'd, with marvel great,
    Why Scots their herald did withhold.
Not any caufe could they conject,   37
    But all furmifes were deferr'd,
And fage advice was clean defect
    Till they the Scottifh herald heard,

Wherefore as foon as Phœbus fair   38
 Dame Luna's light and ftars did ftain,
And burning in the fiery chair
 His ftartling fteed hal'd forth amain,
The earl and all his council fage   39
 On horfeback then they hied around,
And every man did bring his page
 To hold their horfes in that ftound.
But when they ftept within the ftreet,   40
 The Scot was fcarce from cabbage got,
Where he the Englifh lords did greet
 With little court'fie, like a Scot.
Which done, th' earl did then command   41
 His meffage he fhould manifeft.
Then Ilay haftly out of hand
 His chiefeft charge anon expreft :
" My fovereign lord," quoth he, " king Jame,   42
 " Would of your honour gladly hear,
" If Rougecroix was charg'd in your name
 " Such bold words to his grace to bear.
" My mafter doth miftruft his words   43
 " With leafing to be underlay'd
" Likewife do all our peerlefs lords ;"
 Then foon he told what Rougecroix faid.
Quo' th' earl, " What does thy mafter mean,   44
 " Of herald ours to make fuch dread ?
" His meffage for to forge or feign
 " Of leafing we do ftand no need.

" Our herald's words we'll juftify,   45
   " For verity he did reveal ;
" His writings eke the fame will try
   "Which of our arms do bear the feal.
" Wherefore I of thy mafter mufe,   46
   " Our herald why he handleth fo
" And 'gainft all reafon doth refufe
   " Our meffage to make anfwer to."
Then Ilay to the earl reply'd,   47
   " I fay," quoth he, " fo faid my lord,
" And to your meffage at this tide
   " I fhall make anfwer word for word :
" And for Ford Caftle, firft of all,   48
   " Which to preferve you do make fuit
" To fave the fame from fire or fall,
   " My mafter thereto biddeth mute.
" And for the owner of the fort,   49
   " Who William Heron hath to name,
" My mafter fays to fhow you fhort,
   " He will not anfwer to the fame.
" For Johnftone, and Sir Sandy Hume,   50
   " Sir Richard Hume and William Carr,
" Our prince himfelf in perfon's come
   " Them to redeem by dint of war.
" If ye your meffage dare make good   51
   " On Friday next in feild to fight,
" My mafter with a manful mood
   " To mighty Jove has promif'd plight,

" For to abide the battle bold   52
   " And give your folks fighting their fill,
" And that your lordship show I should
   " So grateful be his grace until,
" As any earl all England thorough ;   53
   " For if he had such message sent,
" He being at home in Edinborough,
   " He would have answered your intent.
" Now if with dint of sword ye dare   54
   " Abide his grace in battle bold
" On Friday next, he craves no far.
   " My message whole now I have told."--
A thousand thanks earl Surrey there   55
   Unto the royal king did yeild,
Whose princely heart did not forbear
   So simple a lord to meet in feild.
And then a valiant vow he plight,   56
   That he in battle bold would 'bide
And on prefixed day to fight ;
   Which done, he did command that tide
The Scottish herald, Ilay clept,   57
   A season there he should sojourn
And in safe custody be kept,
   Till time that Rougecroix did return.
When as the herald Ilay heard,   58
   He straight to the king his servant sent,
Who to his grace all things declar'd
   With the earl's answer and intent.

The king then Rougecroix did difcharge   59
   Who hy'd home to the earl in haft ;
Then Ilay was let go at large
   When Rougecroix came who was kept faft.
Then Rougecroix did make true report   60
   To th' earl and captains, in like cafe
As he had feen, and in what fort
   The Scottifh king encamped was.
Even on the height of Floddon hill,   61
   Where down below his ord'nance lay,
So ftrong that no man's cunning fkill
   To fight with him could find a way.
Such mountains fteep, fuch craggy hills   62
   His army on th' one fide inclofe ;
The other fide great grizzly gills
   Did fence with fenny mire and mofs.
Which when the earl had underftood,   63
   He council crav'd of his captains all,
Who bad fet forth with manful mood
   And take fuch fortune as would fall ;
Whereto the earl did foon confent   64
   And quickly called for a guide,
Left by the way he harm might hent :
   But hark what happened that tide.

THE SEVENTH FIT.

When th' army preſt was to proceed,   1
  All 'rayed in ranks, ready to fight,
Came ſcowring all in ſcarlet red,
  With luſty lance, a horſeman light ;
His face with vailed vizard hid,   2
  Thus plainly I have heard report,
Who radly by the ranks did ride
  And to the earl did ſtraight reſort.
All th' army marvel'd at this man,   3
  To ſee him ride in ſuch array ;
But what he was, or whence he came,
  No knight there was could certain ſay.
When he the earl of Surrey ſaw,   4
  From ſaddle light he leaped there,
And down on knees did lout full low,
  Holding in hand his horſe and ſpeare.
And on this ſort he ſilence brake :   5
  " My lord," quoth he, "grant me ſome grace !
" Pardon my life for pity's ſake,
  "You have the prince's power and place !
" Grant at your hand I grace may have,   6
  " Freely forgive me mine offence !
" Perchance ye ſhortly ſhall perceive
  "Your kindneſs I may recompenſe."

Quoth th' earl then, " Note us thy name ;   7
  " Belike thou'ft done fome heinous deed,
" And dare not fhew thy face for fhame.
  " What is thy fact ?   Declare with fpeed !
" If thou haft wrought fome treafon, tell,   8
  " Or Englifh blood by murther fpilt,
" Or thou haft been fome rude rebell,—
  " Elfe we will pardon thee thy guilt."
Then to the earl he did reply   9
  And fay, " My lord, for offence fuch
" The total world I do defy ;
  " With treafon me no man can touch.
" I grant indeed I wrong have wrought,   10
  " Yet difobedience was the worft ;
" Elfe I am clear from deed or thought,
  " And extreams me thereto have forc'd.
" And as for murth'ring Englifh men,   11
  " I never hurt man, maid, or wife ;
" Howbeit, Scots fome nine or ten
  " At leaft I have bereft of life.
" Elfe I in time of wealth or want   12
  " Still to my king perfifted true.
" Wherefore good lord, my life do grant ;
  " My name then fhortly I fhall fhew."
" Quoth the earl then, " Pluck up thy heart, 13
  " Thou feems to be no perfon prave.
" Stand up at once ; lay dread apart :
  " Thy pardon free here fhalt thou have.

"Thou feems to be a man indeed,   14
    "And of thy hands hardy and wight;
"Of fuch a man we fhall ftand in need
    "Perchance, on Friday next, at night."
Then on his feet he ftarts up ftraight   15
    And thank'd the earl at that good tide;
Then on his horfe he leaped light,
    Saying, "My lord, ye lack a guide.
"But I fhall you conduct full ftraight   16
    "To where the Scots encamped are;
"I know of old the Scottifh fleight
    "And crafty ftratagems of war;
"Thereto experience hath me taught.   17
    "Now fhall I fhow you who I am:
"On borders here I was upbrought,
    "And Baftard Heron is my name."—
"What!" quoth the earl, "Baftard Heron!   18
    "He dyed at leaft now two year fince
"Betwixt Newark and Northampton;
    "He perifht through the peftilence.
"Our king to death had deem'd the man,   19
    "'Caufe he the Scottifh warden flew,
"And on our borders firft began
    "Thefe raging wars for to renew.
"But God his purpofe did prevent,   20
    "For he dyed of the plague, to prove.
"The king did fince his death lament,
    "He wond'rous well the man did love.

"Would God, thy tale were true this tide,   21
  "Thou Baſtard Heron might be found :
"Thou in this gate ſhould be our guide ;
  "I wot right well thou knows the ground."—
"I am the ſame," ſaid he again,   22
And therewith did unfold his face ;
Each perfon then perceived plain.
  That done, he open'd all the caſe.
Quoth he, "When I the Scots' warden   23
  "Had with my blade bereft of breath,
"I wiſt well I ſhould get no pardon,
  "But ſure I was to ſuffer death.
"In haſte King Henry for me ſent,   24
  "To whom I durſt not diſobey ;
"So towards London ſtraight I went.
  "But hark what wile I wrought by th' way ;
"I nought but truth to you ſhall note :   25
  "That time in many a town and borough
"The peſtilence was raging hot.
  "And raging reigned all England thorough.
"So coming to a certain town,   26
  "I ſaid I was infected ſore ;
"And in a lodge they laid me down,
  "Where company I had no more
"But my own ſecret ſervants three ;   27
  "For townsmen 'fraid for fear they watched.
"So in that ſtead no more ſtaid I,
  "But homeward by the dark deſpatched.

" My fervants fecretly that night   28
    " Did frame a corpfe in cunning fort,
" And on the morrow, foon 'twas light,
    " My death did ruefully report.

" And fo my fervants foon that morn   29
    " The corpfe to bury made them bown,
" Crying ' Alas !' like men forlorn,
    " And feem'd for forrow to fall down.

" The corpfe they cunningly convey'd,   30
    " And caufed the bells aloud be rung,
" And money to the prieft they paid,
    " And fervice for my foul was fung.

" Which done, they tidings ftraight did bring 31
    " Unto King Henry I was dead.
" Chrift have his foul, then faid the king,
    " For fure he fhould have loft his head,

" If he up to the court had come :   32
    " I promif'd had fo by Saint Paul.
" But fince God did prevent our doom,
    " Almighty Chrift forgive his foul.

" To manfion mine I came at laft   33
    " By journeys nimbly all by night ;
" And now two years or more are paft
    " Since open I appear'd in fight.

" No wight did weet but I was dead,   34
    " Save my three fervants and my wife ;
" Now am I ftart up in this ftead,
    " And come again from death to life."—

Which faid, the lords and captains fam   35
    From laughing loud could not refrain,
To hear his gand they had good gam.
    And of his welfare all were fain ;
Whofe policy they had perceiv'd,   36
    And oftentimes his truth had tried ;
Which was the caufe fo fore they crav'd
    This Heron brave to be their guide.
Then forth before he fiercely flew ;   37
    The borderers bold to him they draw.
The total army did enfue
    And came that night to Wooler-Haugh.
There th' Englifh lords did lodge their hoft,   38
    Becaufe the place was plain and dry,
And was within fix miles at moft
    Where as their enemies did lie.
The morrow next they all remov'd,   39
    Though weather was both foul and ill,
Along down by a pleafant flood
    Which called is th' Water of Till.
And all that day they view'd in fight   40
    Where as the Scots for battle bode.
Becaufe the day was fpent, that night
    The army lodg'd at Barmoor wood.
Then valiantly with the vanguard,   41
    The morrow next, with mature fkill
The admirall did march forward,
    And paffed o'er th' Water of Till.

At Twizlebridge, with ordinance   42
  And other engines fit for war,
His father forth did eke advance ;
  And at Millfield, from thence not far,
With the rereward the river paſt,   43
  All ready in ranks and battle array.
They had no need more time to waſt,
  For victuals they had none that day ;
But black faſting, as they were born,   44
  From fleſh or fiſh, or other food ;
Drink had they none two days before,
  But water wan in running flood.
Yet they ſuch ſteadful faiths did bear   45
  Unto their king and native land,
Each one to t'other then did ſwear
  'Gainſt foes to fight while they could ſtand,
And never flee while life did laſt,   46
  But rather die by dint of ſword.
Thus over plains and hills they paſt,
  Until they came to Sandiford,
A brook of breadth a taylor's yerd,   47
  Where th' earl of Surrey thus did ſay :
" Good fellow-ſoldiers, be not fear'd,
  " But fight it out like men this day.
" Like Engliſhmen now play your parts,   48
  " Beſtow your ſtrokes with ſtomach bold ;
" Ye know the Scottiſh coward hearts,
  " And how we ſcourged them of old.

" Strike but three ſtrokes with ſtomachs ſtout, 49
    " And ſhoot each man ſharp arrows three,
" And you ſhall ſee without all doubt
    " The ſcoulding Scots begin to flee.
" Think on your country's common wealth,   50
    " In what eſtate the fame ſhall ſtand ;
" To Engliſhmen no hope of health
    " If Scots do get the upper hand.
" If we ſhould not them boldly bide,   51
    " But beaſtlike backs of them ſhould turn,
" All England north, from Trent to Tweed,
    " The haughty Scots would harry and burn.
" Your faithful wives, your daughters pure, 52
    " They would not ſtick for to defile ;
" Of life none could be ſafe or ſure,
    " But murther'd be by villains vile.
" But if ye'll fight like ſoldiers fierce,   53
    " So that by force we win the feild,
" My tongue cannot tell and rehearſe
    " What plenteous ſpoil we then ſhall weild.
" Beſides all that, perpetual praiſe   54
    " Throughout all ages we ſhall gain,
" And quietly drive forth our days,
    " And in perduring peace remain."
All ſam the ſoldiers then replied,   55
    And to the earl they promiſ'd plight,
There on that bent boldly to bide,
    And never flee but fiercely fight.

BATTLES FOUGHT IN FLODDON FIELD,

Taken from an
Ancient Manuscript which was transcribed by
Mr. Richard Guy,
late Schoolmaster in Ingleton, Yorkshire.

Part IV.

THE EIGHTH FIT.

(To a pleasant Tune.)

Then marched forth the men of war,   1
  And every band their banner shew'd,
And trumpets hoarse were heard afar,
  And glift'ring harnefs shining view'd.
Thus they paft forth upon the plain,   2
  And ftraight forth by a valley low,
Where up above, on the mountain,
  The Scots' army in fight they faw,
Whom they did leave on the left hand,   3
  And paft forth on the funny fide ;
Till 'twixt the Scots and Scottifh land
  They were conducted by their guide.

Now all this while the king of Scots   4
    Beheld them fair before his eyen ;
Within his mind drove many doubts,
    Mufing what th' Englifhmen did mean.
Giles Mufgrave[102] was a guileful Greek,   5
    And friend familiar with the king,
Who faid, " Sir king, if ye do feek
    " To know the Englifhmen's meaning,
" Ye better notice none can have   6
    " Than that which I to you fhall tell ;
" What they forecaft I full conceive,
    " I know their purpofe paffing well.
" Your marches they mean for to fack,   7
    " And borders yours to harry and burn ;
" Wherefore it's beft that we go back,
    " From fuch intent them for to turn."
This Mufgrave was a man of fkill,   8
    And fpake this for a policy,
To caufe the king come down the hill,
    That fo the battle tried might be.
The king gave credit to his words,   9
    Trufting his talk was void of traine ;
He with confent of all his lords
    Did march with fpeed down to the plaine.
By north there was another hill,   10
    Which Branxton hill is call'd by name ;
The Scots anon did fcoure there till,
    Left th' Englifhmen fhould get the fame.

The litter which they left behind,   11
　　And other filth, on fire they fet
Whofe dufty fmoak the wraftling wind
　　E'en ftraight between the armies bet.
Still on the height the Scots them held ;   12
　　The Englifhmen march on below ;
The fmothering fmoak the light fo feal'd
　　That neither army th' other faw.
At length the weather waxed clear,   13
　　And fmoak confum'd within a while ;
Now both the hofts in diftance were
　　Not paft a quarter of a mile.
Then th' admirall did plain afpeĉt   14
　　The Scots array'd in battles four ;
The man was fage and circumfpeĉt,
　　And foon perceived that his power
So great a ftrength could not gainftand ;   15
　　Wherefore he to his father fent,
Defiring him, ftraight out of hand
　　With th' rereward ready to be bent,
And join with him in equal ground :   16
　　Whereto the earl agreed anon.
Then drums ftruck up with dreadful found,
　　And trumpets blew with doleful tone.
Then founding bows were foon upbent ;   17
　　Some did their arrows fharp uptake ;
Some did in hand their halberts hent ;
　　Some rufty bills did ruffling fhake.

Then ord'nance great anon outbraſt   18
   On either ſide, with thundering thumps,
And roaring guns with fire faſt
   Then levell'd out great leaden lumps.
With rumbling rage thus Vulcan's art   19
   Began this feild and fearful fight ;
But the arch-gunner on th' Engliſh part
   The maſter Scot did mark ſo right,
That he with bullet braſt his brain,   20
   And hurl'd his heels his head above.
Then pip'd he ſuch a peal again,
   The Scots he from their ord'nance drove.
So by the Scots' artillery   21
   The Engliſhmen no harm did hent ;
But the Engliſh gunner grievouſly
   Them tennis-balls he fouſing ſent,
Into the midſt of th' enemy's ranks,   22
   Where they with ragious claps down ruſh'd,
Some ſhouting laid with broken ſhanks,
   Some crying laid with members cruſh'd.
Thus th' Engliſhmen with bombard ſhot   23
   Their foes on heaps down thick they threw ;
But yet the Scots with ſtomachs ſtout
   Their broken ranks did ſtill renew.
And when the roaring guns did ceaſe,   24
   To handy ſtrokes they hied apace,
And with their total power preaſe
   To join with enemy face to face.

The Englishmen their feather'd flight   25
  Sent out anon from sounding bow,
Which wounded many a warlike wight,
  And many a groom to ground did throw.
The grey goose wing did work such grief,   26
  And did the Scots so scour and skail ;
For in their battle, to be brief,
  They rattling flew as rank as hail.
That many a soldier on the soil   27
  Lay dead that day through dint of dart ;
The arrows keen kept such a coil,
  And wounded many a wight his heart,
And pierc'd the scalp of many a Scot,   28
  So that on ground they groaning fell ;
Some had his shoulder quite through shot ;
  Some leaving life did loudly yell ;
Some from his leg the lance would pull ;   29
  Some through his stomach sore was stickt ;
Some bleeding bellow'd like a bull ;
  Some were through privy members prickt.
But yet the Scots still stout did stand   30
  Till arrow shot at last was done,
And plied apace to strokes of hand,
  And at the last did battle join.
Then on the English part with speed   31
  The bills stept forth and bows went back ;
The moorish pikes and mells of lead
  Did deal there many a dreadful thwack.

The Englifhmen ftretcht eaft and weft,   32
    And fouthward did their faces fet ;
The Scotchmen northward proudly preft,
    And manfully their foes they met.
Firft weftward of a wing there was   33
    Sir Edward Howard captain chief,
With whom did pafs in equal mace
    Sir Bryan Tunftall, to be brief ;
With whom encounter'd a ftrong Scot   34
    Which was the king's chief chamberlain,
Lord Hume[29] by name, of courage hot,
    Who manfully march'd them again.
Ten thoufand Scots, well tried and told,   35
    Under his ftandard ftout he led ;
When th' Englifhmen did them behold,
    For fear at firft they would have fled,
Had not the valiant Tunftall been,   36
    Who ftill ftept on with ftomach ftout,
Crying, " Come on, good countrymen,
    " Now fiercely let us fight it out !
" Let not the number of our foes   37
    " Your manful hearts minifh or fhock ;
" Let ne'er be laid unto our nofe,
    " That Scotchmen made us turn our back.
" Like doughty lads, let's rather dye,   38
    " And from our blood take all rebuke ;
" With edged tools now let us try."—
    Then from the earth he mould uptook,

And did the fame in mouth receive   39
   In token of his Maker dear,
Which, when his people did perceive
   His valiant heart, renew'd their chear.
Then firft before in foremoft 'ray   40
   The trufty Tunftall bold forth fprung;
His ftomach could no longer ftay,
   But thund'ring thruft into the throng.
And as true men did make report,   41
   In prefent place which did onlook,
He was the firft, for to be fhort,
   On th' Englifh part that proffer'd ftroke.
All thofe that he with halbert caught   42
   He made to ftagger in that ftound,
And many a groom to ground he brought,
   And dealt there many a deadly wound;
And foreward ftill 'gainft foes he flew,   43
   And thrafhing turn'd them all to teene;
Where he a noble Scotchman flew,
   Which called was Sir Malkin Keene[103];
And ftill his foes purfued faft,   44
   And weapon in Scotch blood he warm'd,
And flaught'ring lafh'd, till at the laft
   The Scots fo thick about him fwarm'd,
That he from fuccour fever'd was   45
   And from his men which Scots had fkail'd;
Yet for all that he kept his place,
   He fiercely fought and never fail'd;

Till with an edged fword one came   46
    And at his legs below did lafh,
And near a fcore of Scots all fam
    Upon his helmet high did hafh.
Though he could not withftand fuch ftrength, 47
    Yet never would he flee nor yeild ;
Alas ! for want of aid, at length
    He flain was fighting fierce in feild.
Down fell this valiant active knight,   48
    His body great on ground did lye ;
But up to heaven with angels bright
    His golden ghoft did flick'ring flye.
After his fall his people fled,   49
    And all that wing did fall to wrack ;
Some fighting fierce died in that ftead,
    The reft for terror turn'd their back ;
Save Sir Edmond Howard alone,   50
    Who with his ftandard bearer yet,
Seeing his folks all fled and gone,
    In haft to vanguard hyed to get.
But he Scot-free had not fo 'fcap'd,   51
    For why, right hot Sir David Hume
With troop of Scots had him entrapt,
    Had not John Baftard Heron come
With half a fcore of horfemen light,   52
    Crying, " Now Howard have good heart,
" For unto death till we be dight,
    " I promife here to take thy part."

Which heard, then Howard heart updrew,   53
   And with the fpearmen forth he fprung,
And fierce among their foes they flew,
   Where David Hume down dead they flung ;
And many a Scot that ftout did ftand   54
   With dreadful ftroke they did reward.
So Howard through bold Heron's hand
   Came fafe and found to the vanguard,
Where th' admirall, with ftrength extent,   55
   Then in the feild fierce fighting was,
'Gainst whom in battle bold was bent
   Two earls of an antique race :
Th' one Craufford[104] call'd, th' other Montrofs,[105]   56
   Who led twelve thoufand Scotchmen ftrong,
Who manfully met with their foes
   With leaden mells and lances long.
There battering blows made fallets found ;   57
   There many a fturdy ftroke was given,
And many a baron brought to ground,
   And many a banner broad was riven.
But yet in fine, through mighty force,   58
   The admirall quit himfelf fo well
And wrought fo, that the Scots had worfe,
   For down in feild both earls fell.
Then th' earl of Surrey next by eaft   59
   Moft fiercely 'gainft his foes he fought,
'Gainft whom King Jame in perfon preft,
   With banners blazed his battle brought.

Wherein was many a baron bold,   60
  And many a lord of lufty blood,
And trufty knights well tried and told,
  And mitred prelates paffing proud.
With th' earl of Catnefs and Caftell,[106]   61
  The earl of Morton and of Marr,
With Arell, Adell, and Athell
  With Bothwell bold, and of Glenkarr ;[107]
Lord Lovat led a lufty power,   62
  So Cluefton, Inderby, and Rofs ;[108]
Lord Maxwell with his brethren four,
  With Borthwitk, Bargeny, and Forbes ;[109]
Lord Arfkill, Sentclear, and Simpell,[110]   63
  With foldiers tried a mighty fum ;
All with the king came down the hill,
  With Cowell, Kay, and Caddie Hume ;[111]
With captains great and commons ftout,   64
  'Bove twenty thoufand men at leaft,
Which with the king moft fierce on foot
  Againft their foes was then addreft.
The earl of Surrey on th' Englifh fide   65
  Encouraged his foldiers keen,
Crying—" Good fellows, ftrike this tide ;
  " Now let your doughty deeds be feen !"
Then fpears and pikes to work were put,   66
  And blows with bills moft dure were delt,
And many a cap of fteel through cut,
  And fwinging fwaps made many fwelt.

There many a foldier fell in foun,   67
   On either fide with wounds right fore,
And many a ftrong man ftrucken down
   In dying rageoufly did roar.
On one fide death triumphant reign'd   68
   And ftopt their pains as well as groans ;
Of thofe who piercing wounds had gain'd,
   The hills did echo with their moans.

THE NINTH FIT.

Then on the Scottifh part right proud   1
   The earl of Bothwell did outbraft,
And ftepping forth with ftomach good
   Into the enemies' throng did thraft,
And " Bothwell ! Bothwell !" cried bold,   2
   To caufe his foldiers to enfue ;
But there he catcht a welcome cold,
   The Englifhmen ftraight down him threw ;
Thus Haburn[112] through his hardy heart   3
   His fatal fine in conflict found.
Now all this while on either part
   Was dealt full many a deadly wound ;

On either fide were foldiers flain   4
  And ftricken down by ftrength of hand,
That who fhould win none weet might plain ;
  The victory in doubt did ftand,
Till at the laft great Stanley ftout   5
  Came marching up the mountain fteep ;
His folks could hardly faft the foot ;
  But forc'd on hands and feet to creep.
Some from the leg the boot would draw,   6
  That toes might take the better hold,
And fome from foot the fhoe would throw :
  Of true men thus I have been told.
The fweat down from their bodies ran,   7
  And hearts did hop in panting breaft,
Until the mountain top they wan
  In warlike wife, ere Scotsmen wift ;
Where for a fpace brave Stanley ftay'd,   8
  Until his folks had taken breath,
To whom all fam e'en thus he faid :
  " Moft hardy mates, down from this heath
" Againft our foes faft let us hye,   9
  " Our valiant countrymen to aid ;
" With fighting fierce, I fear me, I,
  " Through ling'ring long they be o'erlaid.
" My Lancafhire moft lively wights   10
  " And chofen mates of Chefhire ftrong,
" From founding bows your feather'd flights
  " Let fiercely fly your foes among.

" March down from this high mountain top,   11
 " And brunt of battle let us bide
" With ftomachs ftout ; let's make no ftop,
 " And Stanley ftout will be your guide.
" A fcourge for Scots my father was ;   12
 " He Barwick town from them did gain.
"No doubt but ere this day fhall pafs,
 " His fon like fortune fhall obtain.
" And now the earl of Surrey fore   13
 " The Scots, I fee, befets this tide ;
" Now, fince with foes he fights before,
 " We'll fuddenly fet on their fide."—
The noife then made the mountains ring,   14
 And " Stanley ftout !" they all did crye.
Out went anon the grey goofe wing,
 Amongft the Scots did flick'ring flye ;
And fhowers of arrows fharp were fhot,   15
 They rattling ran as rank as hail,
And pierced the fcalp of many a Scot :
 No fhield or pavifh could prevail.
Although the Scots at Stanley's name   16
 Were 'ftonifht fore, yet ftout they ftood,
And for defence did fiercely frame,
 And arrows' dint with danger bode.
Lord Borthwick, Bargeny, and Forbes,   17
 With them ten thoufand Scotsmen ftrong,
Through death endur'd with danger force ;
 Right ftoutly yet they ftood to 't long.

This when the Stanley ſtout did ſee,   18
   Into the throng he thund'ring thraſt.
" My lovely Lancaſhire lads," quoth he,
   " Down with the Scots! the day we waſt."—
The foes he forc'd to break their 'ray,   19
   And many a life was loſt that while ;
No voice was heard but " Kill and ſlay,"
   Down goes the earl of Argyle ;
The earl of Lenox' luck was like,   20
   He fighting fierce was ſlain that tide ;
Lord Forbes, Bargeny, and Borthwick,
   Upon that bent did breathleſs bide.
And ſo the earl of Huntley's hap   21
   Had been, reſembling to the reſt ;
But that through ſkill he made a 'ſcape,
   With an Engliſh blade he had been bleſt.
But he by hap had horſe at hand,   22
   On which he ſcouring 'ſcapt away ;
Elſe doubtleſs as the caſe did ſtand,
   On Floddon hill he'd dyed that day.
After theſe lords were dead or fled,   23
   The companies, left captainleſs,
Being ſore aſtoniſht in that ſtead,
   Did fall to flight, both more or leſs ;
Whom Stanley with his total ſtrength   24
   Purſued right ſore down on the plain,
Where on the King he light at length
   Which fighting was with all his main.

When his approach the King perceiv'd,   25
    With ſtomach ſtout he him withſtood ;
His Scots right bravely them behav'd
    And boldly there the battle bode,
Then ſhowers of arrows fierce outbroke,   26
    And each part did ſo pierce and gall,
That ere they came to handy ſtroke,
    A number great on ground did fall.
The King himſelf was wounded ſore,   27
    An arrow fierce in's forehead light,
That hardly he could fight any more,
    The blood ſo blemiſhed his ſight.
Yet like a warrior ſtout he ſtay'd,   28
    And fiercely did exhort that tide
His men to be nothing difmay'd,
    But battle boldly there to bide.
" Fight on, my men," the King then ſaid,   29
    "Yet fortune ſhe may turn the ſcale,
" And at my wounds be not difmay'd,
    " Nor ever let your courage fail."—
Thus dying did he brave appear,   3ſi
    Till ſhades of death did cloſe his eyes ;
Till then he did his ſoldiers chear
    And raiſe their courage to the ſkies.
But what avail'd his valour great,   31
    Or bold device ?   All was but vain :
His captains keen fail'd at his feet,
    And ſtandard bearer down was ſlain.

Th' archbifhop of St. Andrew brave,[57]   32
    King Jame his fon in bafe begot,
That doleful day did death receive
    With many a lufty lordlike Scot,
Lord Erfkine, Sinclair, and Sempel,   33
    Morton, and Fair, for all their power,
The earl of Erroll and Athell,
    Lord Maxwell with his brethren four.
And laft of all amongft the lave   34
    King Jame himfelf to death was brought;
Yet by whofe hands none could perceive,
    But Stanley ftill moft like was thought.
After the King and captains flain,   35
    The commons ftraight did fall to ground;
The Englifhmen purfued amain
    And never ceaf'd till fun went down.
Then the earl Surrey caufed to found   36
    A trumpet to retreat anon,
And captains cauf'd to keep their ground
    Till morrow next while night was gone.
And th' Englifh foldiers all that night,   37
    Although they weary were with toil,
The Scotsmen coftly flain in fight
    Of jewels rich fpar'd not to fpoil.
The corpfe of many a worthy wight   38
    They uncaf'd of his comely 'ray,
And many a baron brave and knight
    Their bodies there all naked lay.

The carcafe of the king himfelf   39
   Naked was left as it was born ;
The earl could not know it fo well,
   Searching the fame upon the morn ;
Till the Lord Dacres at the laft   40
   By certain figns did him bewray ;
The corpfe then in a cart being caft,
   They to Newcaftle did convey.
The certain fum being fearched out,   41
   Twelve thoufand Scots died in that ftead ;
On th' Englifh fide were flain about
   Some fifteen hundred as we read ;
Yet never a nobleman of fame,   42
   But Bryan Tunftall bold, alas,
Whofe corpfe home to his burial came
   With worfhip great, as worthy was.
Great ftore of guns and warlike gear   43
   Where as the field was fought was found,
Which they to Barwick then, being near,
   And to Newcaftle carried round.
This feild was fought in September,   44
   In chronicles as may be feen,
In th' year of God, as I remember,
   Thoufand three hundred and thirteen.

THE END.

ANNOTATIONS

AND

𝔚𝔞𝔯𝔦𝔬𝔲𝔰 𝔚𝔢𝔞𝔡𝔦𝔫𝔤𝔰.

ABBREVIATIONS:
W. for Weber; L. for Lambe; B. for Beason; F. for Fragments;
A.S. for Anglo-Saxon.

The marginal numbers refer to the Stanzas.

FIT I.

1.—The word FIT, from the Anglo-Saxon FITTE=song, FITTIAN =sing, is equivalent to canto, division. Thomas Gent mistook it for fight.

This poem being evidently part of a larger work dealing with the French wars in the early part of Henry VIII's reign, the transcriber of this portion of the original manuscript found it necessary to insert in this stanza the king's name, "King Henry's affairs," and it was so printed by both Lambe and Weber. The latter has "wars" for "jars."

2.—FIELD, FEILD, and FEILDE, throughout this poem has the signification of battle, battle-field, and camp; compare Shakespeare, *Henry VI.*, i. 1. This stanza is thus given by W. :—

> A fearful field in verse to frame
> I mean, if that to mark ye list ;
> O Floddon Mount, thy fearful name
> Doth sore affray my trembling fist.

3.—"Thou God of War !" W. has "Almighty Mars !"
The same editor inserts here the following stanza :—

> You Muses all, my mind incense,
> And thou, Polymnia, most prudent,
> Lest Nemesis for each offense
> With poet's rod make me repent."

6.—The last three lines of this stanza read in W.—

> The haughty Howard's noble act ?
> Though paper none did make report,
> Fame would not fail such noble fact."

7.—"Wond'rous man ;" W. has—
          stiff in stour
Thou imp of Mars, thy worthy meeds
Who can discourse with due honour,
Or paint with praise thy valiant deeds ?

9.—BLAZ'D=blazoned, adorned, figured, from the French
BLASONNER.
BRAVELY, used here in both its meanings, viz. gaudily
(blaz'd), and courageously (borne).
FORLORNE = taken off ; compare Spenser's *Faerie Queen*,
" Is all his force forlorn."

11.—TRANSFLEET = sail across. I am unable to meet with
another instance of this boldly coined word.
DISEASE=trouble.

12.—The first three lines in W. are :—
    For he, perusing in presence
    Of English kings their battles bold,
    He saw how Scots in their absence

This stanza is evidently one of those to which Gent alludes
when he says : " In the first part of these battles it was
very hard to make out the copy, it being much obliterated,
and the leaves worn out in many places, so that some
words were forced to be added.

13.—LEAST=lest.
TEENE = harm, injury ; from the A.S. TEONA. Shakespeare has " a week of teen," *Richard III. iv.* 1.

14.—BAD, old perfect of to bid, to command. The A.S. form
of the verb is BEODAN, BEAD, GEBODEN.

17.—BOW=bowman, archer.

18.—MACK = equal, match, kind. A.S. MACA, GEMACA.
" What mack o' thing's yon ? "=What kind of a thing is
that (Craven dialect.)

20.—LUSTY=stout, vigorous.

23.—ABODE=stay. " My long abode," *Merchant of Venice, ii.* 9.

25.—EARL. W. has :—
    The earl then his tenants tall
    Martially in musters did elect,
which is a better reading than Gent's. The word EARL is
here, as in many other parts of the ballad, a dissyllable,
the initial e being sounded as y. This fact is a proof

that the writer of the ballad was a native of one of the three Northumbrian counties, in which alone the Norse or Danish form VARL. was and is still used, whilst in the rest of the kingdom the monosyllabic A.S. EORL was heard.

26.—GEER=gear.

HOUSE OF FENCE = fortified building. We find in Sir Walter Scott's *Monastery* a good description of such forts: "In each village or town were several small towers, having battlements projecting over the side walls, and usually an advanced angle or two, with shot-holes for flanking the doorway, which was also defended by a strong door of oak, and often by an exterior door of iron. These small peel-houses were ordinarily inhabited by the principal fuars (feudal tenants) and their families; but upon the alarm of approaching danger, the whole inhabitants thronged from their own miserable cottages, which were situated around, to garrison these points of defence."

27.—HIS DISTRESS = to harass him.

28.—STREET=road; A.S. straet.
"To run," is "to prick" in W.
"He knew of it," is "he straight did weet" in W.

29.—LIGHT=alighted.
W. has "wapping was" for "was nimbly;" and "bruit abroad" for "all abroad."
BLAZ'D=published; see gloss to stanza 9, ante.

30.—"Forced was;" W. has more correctly "fared was"=had gone.
"Into complaisance" is "to his obeysance" in W.

31.—STILL AS=whenever.

34.—BAND=bond.

40.—SONE=soon.

41.—"Lewis chosen" is "Lewis, your cousin" in W.
W. has "hing" for "spring."

3.—W. has "you see what damage," for "you know what hurt."

44.—GRIEF=difficulty.

46.—JOULT-HEAD = with bloated heads; derived from JOLE = face or cheek, the etymology of which is uncertain, though probability points to the A.S. CEAFL=jaw. To this same root we should refer the modern adjective JOLLY as applied to personal appearance, rather than to the French JOLIF.

BURSTEN = ruptured ; suffering from hernia.

FREERS = friars.

47.—SHIVES=slices. The A.S. form SHIVERE occurs in Chaucer. MILLNERS=millers.

CLERKS = clerici.

The last two lines of this stanza are a very evident reminiscence of " The Reeves' Tale " in Chaucer.

49.—BODWORD=message, from BODE=messenger. There is nothing "ominous" about this word as Lambe supposes.

51.—W.— There is an earl, of antique race,
       Passing in pride and costly array ;
    In his banner brave he displays
       A halfmoon in gold glist'ring gay.

53.—TALBOT=hound ; beagle. The supporters of the earl of Shrewsbury's arms are two talbots argent.

TYKE=dog ; terrier.

SKRIKE = shriek ; Danish SKRIGE. The word is still used in the northern dialects.

57.—LAVE = remainder. Provincial word of the north-eastern counties.

58.—PLUMP=cluster. W. has " clump."

BOYST'ROUS = bellowing.

59.—HIGHT = named. A.S. HATAN, HEHT, HET.—German HEISSEN.—The disuse in modern English of this exceedingly useful word in its two meanings of " to bid " and " to be named " is much to be deplored.

HOLD=wager ; stake.

60.—STOMACH throughout this poem is used in the signification of courage.

62.—HABERGEON=hauberk, neck-piece of armour.

NAGGS = steeds.

WAXEN=grown.

64.—W. has "and plyed" for " complying."

65.—BIDE=stay.

The first line reads thus in W.—
       With that on Lyon loud he cried.

67.—W. has the fourth line thus :—
  And make from me full defiance.

69.—HAL'D=hoisted.

 W.—Then Lyon made him boun lightly,
  And with his coat of arms him deck'd ;
  He haled up sail right heartily
  And towards France his way direct.

FIT II.

1.—W. gives the second line thus :—
  Which pricking posts apace did bear.

3.—MELL=mace.

 GRISLY=horrible.

 GISARINGS = halberts; pole-axes. The word is of
 Anglo-Norman origin, and occurs in Chaucer under the
 form GYSARME.

4.—PIKEFORKS=two-pronged pikes.

6.—W.— The tillmen tough their teams could take
  And to hard harness them conflate ;
  One of a share can shortly make
  A sallet for to save his pate.

8.—W.— Whereof the king, in heart full fain
  His men had all things ready made,
  Did then command his chamberlain
  In England for to make a raid.

9.—HAST=haste.
 The last two lines are given in W. thus :—
  Within the English borders brast
  With full eight thousand men and moe.

11.—LOON=rascal.
 The third line reads thus in W.—
  Some coursers got, some geldings good.

12.—W.— Most stately halls, and houses gay,
  And buildings brave, they boldly burned ;
  And with a mighty spoil and prey,
  Toward Scotland they straight returned.

13, 14, 15, & 16 do not occur in the MS. from which W. took
  his edition. They are evidently an interpolation by

the copyist from whose transcript Gent took his edition,
and who thereby gives us a clue to his own place of origin.

15.—Eye is still pronounced ee in the northern dialects, and
makes therefore a correct rhyme to "piety."

17.—Rout = rush, multitude; W. has "road."

18.—W. has "all their rout" for "horse and foot."

19.—Ken = know. German, kennen
     Coasts = ground, territory. W. has "course."

20.—Scouring = passing rapidly.
     Pricked = galloped.
     "Out of their way," W. has "clear out of 'ray."

21.—Anon = presently.

22.—Spells = splinters. This term is commonly used in all
     the northern counties.

23.—Extend = keep up.

26.—W.— For prickers him so nigh pursued,
         His banner bearer down they bet;
     And all the prey and spoil rescued,
         Besides a sort of geldings get.

27.—W.— Six hundred Scots lay slain on ground,
         Five hundred prisoners and more;
     Of Englishmen slain in that stound,
         The number was not past threescore.

28.—W.—   The day still black with Scottish blood!
         As diverse old men yet do tell,
         The Scots call it the devilish road.

30.—Terwin = Terouanne in Picardy.
     "Bow'd him low;" W. "louring low."

31.—W.— The king he reverently gan greet,
         And took to him his letters large;
     His master's mind he let him weet,
         And did his message whole discharge.
     Discharge = unfold, declare.

33.—"Raise," W. "cease.—"stay," W. "eke."
     The third line is given thus by W. :—
         Or else he with a mighty press.

35.—"Sires never brave," W. "predecessors prave" i.e. de-
     praved.

36.—Fourth line, W. "And turn each truthless guest to teen."
WIGHT = fellow.

38.—First line, W. "Which will withstand him stiff in stour."

39.—"Mad," W. "wood." The latter is the older form.

40.—"Harrass," W. "harry."

41.—"Union make," W. "loveday take."

42.—"Banishing all fears," W. "fast of full defiance."

43.—Last two lines in W.—
"Then homewards he away gan wend,
And towards Scotland forth he far'd.

45.—BENT = ready.

46.—Last line in W.—All that was done straightway he wist.

48.—"Truth," W. "sooth. "Raise for to engage ;" W. "soon
to fee and wage."

49.—W.— Which when the earl understood,
His letters fast he forth did dress
Unto each man of noble blood,
To have their men in readiness.

50.—"tell," W. "eke." "Valiant men," W. "warlike wights."

51.—Third line, W.—"Which to his bidding soon was bent."

52.—CULVERINES. The culverine was one of the earlier forms
of cannon, generally an 18 pounder, of very great length,
and weighing 50 cwt.
"Mortars," W. has "cortals;" Lambe (after Gent) has
"portals," with the suggestion that perhaps "portcullices"
were meant. The idea of carrying "portcullices" amongst
the baggage of an army, is worthy of a Northumbrian
country vicar and truly good man. The term "mortar,"
at the time when this poem was written, began to be used
side by side with the older term "bumbard," which it
afterwards superseded.
STEE = ladder, hurdle. A northern dialect word, still
in use. Lambe's gloss of "steed" is inadmissible.
"Great" in the north-eastern dialects becomes "gert,"
and may therefore be allowed to rhyme with "cart."

53.—"The noble Lord then," W. "That done, the earl."

54.—"Keep," W. "beat." Fourth line in W.—
Till the king came home with their rescue.

55.—"The noble earl did much," W. "The earl Surrey greatly did." "I mean to write," W. "then will I write."

56.—Busked = prepared. Icelandic buasc, bua-sik, and buast = to prepare oneself; see an exhaustive article on this verb in *Latham's Dictionary, s.v. busk.*

57.—W.— When they were all assembled sam
　　　The town of Edenbrough before,
　　Fifty great lords there were of fame,
　　　And barons bold besides great store.

58.—Populous lave = numerous remainder.

59.—"And quite against," W. "contrary to." "That too," W. "specially."

61.—"Mark," W. "prick." Fourth line in W.—
　　　"Ne'er taught them any such a trick."

62.—Learn = teach.
　　Shored = propped. The diagonal cross, resting on two arms, is still called St. Andrew's cross.

63.—"Bold as all," W. "eke, bold as."

　　Beagel rod = pastoral staff, a corruption of the ecclesiastical Latin word baculus. Beagle rods are made of metal, hollow.

64.—Prest = ready. From the old French prest = pret.
　　The third line in W.—
　　　"So that in numbers they did exceed."

65.—"Smile," W. "jet." "Great," W. "huge."
　　The last two lines in W.—
　　　Then soon he bade them forward set,
　　　And eke blaze out his banners bold.

66.—"Train," W. "crew."
　　The last two lines in W.—
　　　Then minstrels mirthed all the land,
　　　And brazen trumpets loud up blew.

67.—W.— Then drums struck up with hideous sound,
　　　And banners bravely waved wide ;
　　　Men might nowhere behold bare ground.

68.—"Graceful," W. "stoutly."

69.—W.— King James thus gorgeously gan ride,
　　　Great pleasure to his peers to see ;
　　　Thus rode this prince, puff'd up with pride,
　　　Whose lofty heart was but too high.

70.—W.— For he thought himself able enough,
　　　　Having so mighty a multitude,
　　　　All Europe then for to pass through,
　　　　And that no hold could him exclude.

71.—" He thought us ;" W. " Nor any."　" An emperour ;" W.
　　" the great Cæsar."

72.—Sophy = emperor of Persia.
　　Soldan = sultan of Turkey.
　　"Work ;" W. " lurk." " valiant ;" W. " lusty."

73.—Second line in W.—And eke for all his haughty heart.
　　" Ghost," W. " bost."　　" And brought," W. " When
　　brought."

74.—W.— Even in the midst of harvest-tide,
　　　　The two-and-twentieth of August,
　　　　Did this proud prince, puft up with pride,
　　　　Into the English borders burst.

75.—Pills = peel-towers, or hill forts.　Welsh pill = fort,
　　stake.　This name is still given to the towers erected on
　　the Scottish borders for defence.　They are square, with
　　turrets at the angles, and the door is sometimes at a height
　　from the ground.　The lower story is usually vaulted, and
　　formed a stable for horses, cattle, &c.　For an account of
　　these old towers, now mostly in ruins, see *Chambers'
　　History of Peeblesshire.*
　　" Stately ;" W. " burly."　" Loons ;" W. " grooms."
　　Fourth line, W.— Or soldiers sacred to Mahound,　*i.e.*
　　Mahomet.
　　Loon = clown.

76.—Third line, W.—" And houses burnt, and bent up gear."

77.—Is not given in Weber's edition.

FIT　III.

1.—W.—　For so the king commanded had,
　　　　To waste and spoil with fire and flame :
　　　　And rifling so by journies rade,
　　　　To Norham castle strait they came.

2.—Bombard = mortar.

4.—Last two lines, W.—
    Alas too lewd'ly he lash'd out,
    And foolishly his ordnance spend.
Lash out=to break out; to be extravagant. *Latham, s.v.*

4.—Fourth line, W.—
    "What should have been his chief succour."
Hal'd=threw.

5.—"Assaults;" W. "hard 'saults."
Extend=brought out.

6.—"Was it not for a;" W. "Had it not been a false."

7.—"Your brave assaults," W. "Your 'deavours here."
Last two lines, W.—
    For all your 'saults and hard besiege
    Of gunshot here ye get no gain.

10.—First line, W.—Then first of all refuse this place.
"Your batteries will," W. "And with brief battery."

11.—Last two lines, W.—
    And ere five piece were shot or mo,
    The walls were all to-razed and rent.

12.—W.— Which made the captain sore agast,
    Seeing the walls down rattling reel'd;
    His weapons all away he cast,
    And to king James simply did yield.

13.—First line, W.—The Scots anon they scoured in.
"Take," W. "bear't."

14.—Fourth line, W.—For his reward ready to look.

15.—"Town," W. "place."
Last two lines, W.—
    The false knave nothing did deny,
    But said a Scotchman born he was

16.—Meek and mild," W. "with words mild."
Third line, W. Quoth he, Still since I was a child.

18.—"Heart," W. "faith."
"Thou never canst," W. "That thou wilt not."

19.—Trace = rope.

20.—W.— What he had said forepast was nought,
    The king's judgment was worthy praise;
    If he in all things had so wrought,
    Belike he had driven forth more days.

21.—"Flying posts," W. "pricking post." "Of Scotland's hosts," W. "with a great host."

23.—W.— That the first day of September,
 Both gentlemen, knights, lords, and squire,
 Unto Newcastle should repair.

24.—W.— Himself set forth in fine array,
 And neither stint, nor staid his foot,
 But strait to Durham took his way.

25.—"Prayers," W. "mass."
 Last two lines, W.—
 Then pray'd the prayer of that place,
 Saint Cuthbert's banner for to bear.

26. —"Repair'd," W. "did draw."

27.—"Valiant," W. "doughty." "Noble," W. "burly."
"Men," W. "wights." "Compleat," W. "replete."

28.—Second line, W.—"Accompanied with his seemly sons."
 ROUT = multitude.
 CLAPPING = booming. Compare the substantive CLAP of thunder, and the Allemannic KLEPFEN (Switzerland and Suabia).

29.—"Soon he went," W. "gan he flit."
 ANWICK = Alnwick, pronounced ANNICK.
 "Travel spent,', W. "weather bit."
 Fourth line, W.—
 Might have the more casement and room.
 ROON=rest. Teutonic RUH. Morris quotes in his *Specimens of Early English* the adjective ROOLESS = restless. In the form ROOM, given by Weber and Lambe (after Gent) there is neither rhyme nor reason.
 "Town," Northumbrian pronunciation "toon," will of course rhyme to "roon."

30.—"With shining," W. "Here silken." "Glittering from afar," W. "high glist'ring afar."

31.—W.— From Lancashire nnd Cheshire fast,
 They to the lusty Stanley drew;
 From Hornby where as he in hast
 Set forward with a comely crew.

33.—CHEAR = mien, face. Compare Italian CERA.

34.—This stanza is not given by Lambe (Gent); an oversight, I suppose, for it exists in all the manuscripts.

IN HARNESS HORSE = harnessed on horseback.
TOOK LITTLE FORCE = lost their comfort.
This and the preceding stanza are amongst the most
beautiful in this poem, full of touching pathos.

35.—Lambe, in pious horror, substituted the word "prayers"
for masses ;" see also stanza 25, ante.
EKE = too, also.

37.—BEDS should of course be BEADS as given by Weber.
OUT is pronounced "oot" in the north eastern dialects,
and therefore may be allowed to rhyme to "foot."

38.—ON HIGHT = on high.

39.—"In yon," W. "is yon." "Did enquire," W. "he did cry."

40.—Second line, W.—"A cock curling as he would crow."
CURLING = bending back.

42.—BLAZE OUT = unfold.

43.—TIDE = time. Norse TID, Allemannic ZIT. The word
is still used in Yorkshire for the commemoration or dedi-
cation feast of the various parishes, degenerated to a
village fair. Compare the German IAHRZEIT. In the
proverb "time and tide wait for no man," we have the
northern and southern equivalent placed together in pun-
ning alliteration. It is questionable whether the concrete
entity "ocean tide" entered at all into the original idea
of the proverb, seeing that FLOOD-TIDE really means
nothing else but FLOOD-TIME, and EBBING-TIDE = time
of ebbing, and that therefore the word TIDES is a mere
equivalent to TIMES.

44.—First line, W.—Then said the Stanley where he stood.
Third line, W.—Be not amazed in your mood.
"Valiant," W. "doughty." "Tho'" W. "For."

45.—First line, W.—Set forward, sirs, then did he say.
Third line, W.—And being sore wearied with the way.

46.—"Flapping wings," W. "wings wapped;" Gent "wrapping
wings."
BARE = bore (could have carried).

47.—W.— At Alnwick while the army increased,
The weather waxt both foul and wet ;
With rain down rattling never ceased,
That every brook burst forth on float.

48.—W.— Such rustling winds, such blust'ring blast,
    Down rushing day and night did sound,
    Which made the earl full sore agast
    His son lord Admiral should be drown'd.

49.—"All his might," W. "main and might."
  Fourth line, W.—His fleet in merry 'ray to 'rive.

50.—W.— Sir Neptune did such friendship shew ;
    And safely then, him and his fleet,
    ·To happy haven did bestow.

51.—Hy'd = hastened. A. S. HIGAN.
  "In arms," W. "at least."

53.—"Divers," W. "many."

54.—"Hasted as," W. "fast busied."

55.—"Truth," W. "sooth."

56.—Hert = heart.

58.—Kist = kissed.
  Eyen, the old plural of eye, still used in various dialects,
   especially in the north.
  Forepast = former.

59.—Sone = soon.

60.—Atchieve = accomplish.
  To pass back = to send back.
  "Counties," W. "countries."

62.—"Fail," W. "flee."
  Fourth line, W.—Thus the earl Surrey did admonish.

63.—Hot = angry.

64.—"Nor ever," W. "Let it ne'er be."

65.—"Governour," W. "lieutenant." "Treacherous," W.
  "scoulding."
  Third Line, W.—Trusting that fiercely without fear.

66.—W.— Think on your father's valiance,
    How fierce he fought at Bosworth-field ;
    Till time that he by Stanley's lance
    With grievous wounds his life did yield !

67.—W.— Would God, quoth he, my brother Edward
    Were here alive this present day !
    No foes there could have made him fear'd
    In camp here like a coward to stay.

70.—"Glorious," W. "worthy."

71.—SWAGE = assuage, to beat down.

72.—W.— Your father's fame then should be 'filed,
    His worthy facts should be forgot ;
    The chief renown eke of your child,
    Your beastish acts should clear outblot.

74.—SPACE = time.

FIT IV.

1.—First two lines, W.—
    Then the earl of Surrey again replied,
    And to his son thus gan he say:

3.—" Great," W. "wise."   " Which way our cards," W. " Our cards them both."

4.—HAP = fortune.
    " Off Brest," Lambe " of breast."

5.—" A living man," W. " man alive."
    Fourth line, W.—
    This end his great boldness him brought.

7.—BET = beaten.

8.—SCRIPTURE = handwriting.

9.—REAVED = bereft.
    GUERDON = recompense;   taken   unaltered   from   the French.

11.—HINGS = hangs. A. S. HINGAN = to hang.   The Craven dialect still has HINGS.

12.—" Fright," W. "fraught."   The former in the signification of " frightened."   The latter of "burdened ;" compare the modern " freighted."

15.—COMPASS CAST = make a forecast.
    TAST = taste.

17.—PUT CASE = supposing.

18.—CONVINCE = overcome, in the meaning of the Latin root VINCERE.

20.—Fourth line, W.—
    And our brave troops how seemly drest.

23.—" Mighty," W. " noble."

24.—" Valiant son," W. " son alone."

26.—PUISSANCE = power. Taken unaltered from the French; frequently used by Shakespeare and Spenser.

27.—BLIN = cease. A.S. BLINNAN = to stop.

29.—TA'EN = taken, still used in all the northern dialects. W. has "drawn," which does not rhyme to slain.

31.—Third line, W.—
    Since yet the fame doth record reeke (*i.e.* bring)
    FACTS = deeds.
    This stanza refers to Henry V. of England.

33.—DIGHT = doomed. A.S. DIHTAN = to prepare, to deck, to set out.
    "Who shall dight your bowr's; sith she's dead," Spenser's Daphnaïda.

34.—STINT = stopped. A.S. STINTAN = to stop, to limit.
    "Stinted pasture," in Yorkshire, is pasturage for a definite number of cattle.

35.—DOLPHIN = Dauphin, or Crown Prince, of France. The title of DAUPHIN (Latin DELPHINUS) was adopted in 1349, by Charles de Valois, grandson of Philippe VI. of France, upon the demise, sine prole, of Humbert II., last duke of Dauphiné, who bequeathed his duchy to the crown of France, on condition that the heir apparent should always be the governor of Dauphiné and assume its arms, the crest of which was a dolphin.
    BET = beat.

38.—First line, W.—If we in field be fighting slain.
    AYE = ever.
    OUT-SOUND = proclaim. The use of verbs with separable prefixes, in exact analogy with modern German use, was very common in our earlier English writers; OUT-HERE, OUT-TOKE, IN-SPRANG, &c., are examples of this use. There is a tendency to its reintroduction into current English observable in the formation of such verbal substantives as OUT-PUT (of coal), INDRAUGHT (of a mine), INGATHERING, INTAKE (reclaimed moorland), &c.

39.—HAST = hasten.

40.—WREAK = avenge. A.S. WRECAN, German RÆCHEN.
    DINT = blow.
    DOLEFUL = smarting; in the meaning of the Latin root DOLOR, pain.
    TILL TIME = until.

41.—CASE = state. W. has "cause."

42.—LIGHT = fall out.
    "That to," W. "we do."

43.—GIVE THE FOIL = to worst.

44.—PASSING = exceedingly.
    "With barons," W. "great barons."

45.—"Whose," Lambe "their."
    "Their ent'ring," W. "ent'ring our."
    "Their charges they shall pay," L. "the charges shall pay
    us."

46.—W.— Such fate shall them befal, I trust,
          As elders theirs have done before ;
        Who into England seld did brust, (SELD = occasion-
          ally)
        But they were brust in battle sore.
    BRUST = burst. The form BRUSSEN is common in the
    West Riding of Yorkshire.

47.—TINMOTH = Tynemouth.   The local pronunciation is
    "Tinmoth."

49.—MACK = make.
    PRICKT = spurred on.

51.—"To looke," L. "may look."
    "All the earls," L. "all the earl's," W. "those earls his."

52.—"It's shame," W. "what shame."

53.—ABASED = downcast, in dread.

54.—"Then Stanley," W. "the Stanley."

55.—LAT = lately, previously.
    "Great," L. & W. "keen."
    "Was now uprais'd," L. "did now upraise."

56.—WEILD = command.

57.—"Was deaf," W. "wext deaf" (WEXT = grew).
    "Would," L. & W. "could."
    "Then did appear," W. "he did uprear."

59.—"Shall make true," L. "truly shall."

FIT V.

2.—" Breast," L. " blood."

4.—First line, W.—Whom doughty lords associated.
Last two lines, W.—
> Lord Ogle, who, as then, did lead
> A lordly band of warlike wights.

5.—CAUL = hood, covering (L " coat").
Third line, W.—
> Who had been shroud in shepherd's EARN.

The emendation CAUL, for which the editor is responsible, appears to him the only rational substitution which can be made for the illegible ms. word which Weber has rendered EARN, Lambe (after Gent) COAT, Benson GARB. The form CALLE, from the Anglo-Norman CALE, hood, occurs already in Chaucer. Spenser has, " when they had despoil'd her tire and caul," explained in the previous line as meaning " stripped her naked all," so that " tire and caul" may not unreasonably be rendered by "inner and outer garments." The word EARN, or YEARN, bears no other meaning than " coagulated milk," which is altogether inadmissible in this passage.

6.—Third line, W.—By friends in this wise was concealed.

7.—DIGHT = doomed.
UPHAND = upperhand.

9.—COASTS = territory.

10.—WORLEDALE, (W, " Whorledale," B. Wharledale "). As the whole of this stanza refers to Staincliff hundred in the West Riding of Yorkshire, comprising the Archdeconery of Craven, in which there is no dale of this name, we are reduced to the assumption, that WHARFEDALE is meant ; otherwise it would be difficult to account for the total absence of the latter from the list of districts enumerated in this part of the poem.

11.—FLESHLY = muscular.
" Well brawn'd their ;" W. " well bound with ;" B. " well browned with."
Second line, L.—Were fit the strongest bows to bend.
BRAWNED = strong, brawny. This very obvious emendation (by the editor) is justified by the ordinary use of this form by our early writers. "Whose mighty brawned

bowrs were wont to rive steele plates ; Spenser, *Faerie Queen*, *i.* 8, 41.
The Horton alluded to in this stanza is Horton-in-Ribblesdale.

12.—STOUR = struggle. A.S. STYRUNG ; Norse STURA, sorrow, disturbance. We find DEDE STOURE = death struggle, in Hampole's *Pricke of Conscience*, line 1821. Lambe's gloss of "dust in motion, metaphorically, battle," is throwing "dust" into the reader's eyes.

13.—RYEDALE. This cannot refer to Ryedale in the Wolds, but must be RAYDALE, south of Bainbridge.
MASSAMSHIRE. The country about Masham bears the name of Massamshire.
NOISTERFIELD. The small district of Nosterfield, in the township of West Stanfield, near Ripon, seems very insignificant in juxtaposition to Netherdale, yet no other identification seems possible.

14.—"Tough," W. "taught."
MITTON FEILD. The extensive district of Mitton on the Ribble and Hodder near Clitheroe.
WEILD = command.

17.—Lambe (after Gent) has here the following stanza :—
> The third part it will more unfold
> The glorious train of heroes bright,
> Such as may please the sage and old,
> And yield to children sweet delight.

This is an unwarranted interpolation, made by Gent in order to make a break in this somewhat long fit. It is the more uncalled for, as it is arbitrarily placed in the midst of an enumeration of the leading men of the English army.

17.—L. has the first line—Sir Christopher Ward the next ensued.
"Effingham," L. "Etchingham."
"Metham," L. "Mettham."
"Everingham," W. "Averingham."
W. & L. place commas between the three names, Metham, Sidney, and Everingham. We have followed the Fragments in assigning all the three names to one person.

18.—Second line, L.—These knights who in the vanguard were.

19.—"Howard," B. "Haworth." The northern country-speech still changes d to th ; ex. "Bradforth" for "Bradford ;" "Huthersfield" for "Huddersfield ;" "Atherton" for "Adwalton," &c. Thus Howard will rhyme with "forth."

GAN = began. L. "did."
"Forth," L. "forward."

20.—" Full," L. "now."
Fourth line, L.—And for his sake never think it pain.
LET, from the A.S. LETTAN, to hinder, to oppose, to forbear, must be distinguished from to let, to allow, which
is derived from A.S. LAETAN. The phrase "let for no
pain," means therefore, "do not forbear, however
painful."

21.—WEND (L. "go"), the obsolete infinitive form from which
we have the perfect WENT ; compare the German WENDEN,
to turn.
"Too," W. "though ;" L. "to."
Fourth line, L.—His father dear did render free.

22.—" Swage," L. "sway."

23.—" Eke," L. "too." "Untainted," L. "unspotted."

28.—" Britain," L. "Bretagne." The latter is, of course,
meant.

29.—KIN = family, race.
GARLAND = crown of victory. It may not be superfluous
to note that the original signification of the word
"crown" (Latin "corona") is "wreath."
Third line, L.—When then the carl the crown had gained.

30.—" All," W. "to." "Pure blood unblamed," L. "valiant
blood unstained." "He eke did cause," L. "The king
he caused."

31.—TH'FALLOW FEILD. L. has "Thalian field," with the gloss,
"supposed to be used for Thessalian." W. dissents from
this, but gives no opinion of his own besides suggesting
that it is perhaps a local name now lost. The uninter-
rupted alliteration of this line demands an initial f, with
or without the article, in the word preceding "feild," and
as there is clearly ll in the middle of the word, the word
"fallow" is perhaps the only one which fulfils every
requisite of form and of meaning in this place. FALAW
in Old English, FEALWE in A.S., has the meaning
of "faded," "dreary," "pale." In line 445 of Cursor
Mundi, we find "the falau slogth sal be thi gate, o Para-
dise" (the pale path shall be thy road to heaven), where
pale path stands for death.
"When," W. "where."

32.—Prest=ready, see gloss to st. 64 on page 96.

33.—"Barkeston, " W. "Barkerton," L. "Bruerton," F. "Burker-
ton." "Bygot," L. & W. " Bygod."

34.—" fresh," L. " freest."

35.—" Clartice," L. "Clarvis."
Fare, A.S. faran, German fahren,=to go, to advance.
" feats," F. "faites."

36.—Keen=brave.
"his sire" is omitted in L., probably through a clerical error.

38.—Stiff=proud.
Stoure, see gloss to st. 12, ante.

39.—" did," W. " can."
Seemly kent=beautifully eager.

40.—Doubt = fear.   This affirmative meaning of the verb "to
doubt" is still common in Craven.   "I doubt it'll not
hold " expressed the fear of a churchwarden assisting the
other day in putting up some decorations in a Littondale
church.

41.—Wend, see gloss to stanza 21, ante.
" Wensledale," W. "Wensadale," evidently Wensleydale.
Morton = Morton-upon-Swale.
Moisdale (L. " Morsdale") = Mossdale, near the source
of the river Ure.
" Stour," L. "store," the latter form is a translation of the
former, and is not connected with the "stoure" of stanza
12, ante.

42.—Wensdale, (W. "Weresdale.")   There is some difficulty
in ascertaining the locality referred to.   Being mentioned
in immediate connection with Bishopdale, Coverdale,
Cotterdale and Kidstones, we are driven to the conclusion
that Widdale, near Hawes must be meant.
Cotter End = Cotterdale near Hawes.
Kidson Causey = Kidstones, the upper part of Bishopdale.   Causey, or Causeway, alludes to the formerly much
frequented pass from this dale over the Gavel into
Wharfedale, and over Stake Fell (or Kidstones Fell) into
Raydale.

43.—Mollerstang.   Mallerstang Common is the higher part
of Edendale, south of Kirkby Stephen.

Marsk W. and L.—" Mask" = Marske in Swaledale.

MIDDLETONBY, (W.—" Midleconby,") = Middleton Tyas, near Catterick. The Danish suffix BY, corresponding to the Saxon THORPE, signifies village.

CAM really signifies the summit of any mountain, and occurs in various places in the northern counties. Compare also the suffix KAMM occurring in many Swiss mountain names, ex. Leistkamm (St. Gallen), Weisskamm (Glarus), &c. The mountain alluded to in this stanza is CAM FELL, where the rivers Wharfe and Ribble take their rise, near the Ribblehead Station on the Settle and Carlisle Railway.

44.—SEIMER WATER, the lake which fills the central portion of Raydale, south of Bainbridge. For the legend and popular tradition referring to Seimer Water, see Barker's Three Days of Wensleydale.

45.—" Barkley," L. " Barclay."
" and eke," W. and L. " with."

47.—YEDE (L. "came") is the old preterite of to go, now superseded by " went."
Last two lines, L.—Sir Lionel Piercy, knight of fame,
        Did lead some hundred men well told.

48.—" Ninian," W. " Mimham," F. " Minham."
" Markenfil," W. "Markinfil," F. "Markinfell," L. " Markanville."
" Maundevill," L. " Normanville."

49—" Chestane." L. " Clapham," F. " Chostance."

50.—" Dawbie," L. " Dalby."
" Th' array," L. "array," W. "their 'ray," F. " their way."

52.—" From Copeland's," L. " the Capeland." " Weighty," F. " massy."

54.—"Stanemore," W. & L. "Stainmoor." "Even," F. "kene."
AUSTON = Alston.
GRAVE = hollow. Compare German GRABEN,
" Hexham," W. " Hesham," L. " Heshan," F. " Kesham."

56.—" Houses," L. " Horses" ! surely a misprint.
Last two lines, L.—A baron fair by his birthright,
        And heritage which to him fell.

57.—HINGS = hangs. See gloss to stanza 11, page 102.
Fourth line, L.— From whom true valour fairly springs.

58.—BLIN = cease.
" Laud," L. " praise," W. " land."

79.—STIFF IN STOUR = proud in battle. See gloss to stanza 12, ante.

60.—LIVER = nimble. (W. & F. "lively".)
FELLS = mountains, from the Norse FJELD, used in all the northern counties.

61.—BOUN = going. "Is te boun oo'r t' fells t' neet?" (Craven) = are you going over the hills to-night?

62.—CONNEYSIDE has become modernised recently into CONIS-HEAD Priory.
" Furness," W. & L. " Furneys," F. " Furnace."

64.—RATCHDALE = Rochdale, locally pronounced " Ratchdill."

66.—" Turned out in scores," L. " did turn in furs."

67.—PREST, see gloss to stanza 64, page 96.
" Children," L. " youth."

69.—" Strait with," L. " with strict."
Last line, L.— To know for why these wars did spring.

FIT VI.

2. " The king," W. " his Grace." " Then," L. " there."

3.—"Whereto if," L. "if thus." "Straitway to," L. "immediate."
" His countrymen," " Scotchmen taken."

4.—Third line, W.— And where the king did sore presume.

5.—COMMONS = the common people.
" Pills," W. & L. " piles." For the word PILLS see gloss to stanza 75, page 97.
" Draw," W. " throw."

7.—" Rouge-Croix," W. " Rougecross."

8.—Fourth line, L.— He would prepare himself to fight.

9.—BLESS. Lambe's gloss " wound, from the French blesser,"
though endorsed by Weber, is inadmissible. I believe
that no good instance can be adduced of the use in
English of " to bless" in the sense of "to wound." Nor
is such a meaning required in this stanza: the ironical
force of " gave him a blessing with his blade " explains
itself. In stanza 21 of the 9th fit we have again:—
With an English blade he had been blest.

10.—PREST = ready.
VOUCH = to avouch., to answer for.

13.—FIELD = camp.
"Rouge-Croix was yet," W. "Wherefore Rougecross."

14.—BRAVE = beautiful.

16.—" On knees," L. " on the ground."

17.—First line, L.— With salutations did greet.

18.—" Eke had viewed," L. "also read."
FAR'D = went on.

19.—BREAST = Courage.

20.—Second Line, L.— I swear by sceptre and by crown.
Third line, W.— In faith he shall have fighting enough.

21.—" Part," W. "pass."   " This hill," L. " this same hill."

22.—PATES (L. "heads") = brain-pan, head.
POLLED = lopped off.

23.—" Earl his," L. "earl's whole."   " And audience," L.
"audience being."

24.—" So simple," L. "such a simple."   " Spite," W. "spight."
SCHEDULE = document.
DID SPARE = refrained.

25.—"To use all," W. "with all possible," L. "That they with."
Last line, L— A Scottish herald should address.

26.—To MAKE SURE = to detain.

27.—Second line, L.— That Rouge-Croix should with them
remain.
Fourth line, L.— Their Herald, Ilay called by name.
CLEPT (W. "yclept") = called, from the obsolete infinitive
to CLEPE = to name. to call ; the y in YCLEPT represents
the prefix of the past participle, corresponding to " ge "
in modern German.   A. S. CLYPIAN.

29.—CERTIFYE (L "terrify") = to apprize.

30.—" Eloquent," W. " loquintue ;" " went," W. " drew."

31.—Last line, L.—Whilst clanging trumpets noise did make.

34.—Second line, W.—And lodged then in a little village.
Fourth line, W.—Which might turn to the Scots' advantage.

35.—Fourth line, W.—He strait did on his council call.

36.—TRUMPET = trumpeter.
MUSED = wondered.

37.—CONJECT = conjecture.
DEFECT = wanting.

38.—HAL'D (W. " hail'd ") = drew.
CHAIR = chariot.
AMAIN = forcibly. A.S. ON MÆGNE, by force of hand.

39.—Second line, W.—Who soon on horseback did surround.
HIED = hastened. A.S. HIGAN.
STOUND = time, hour. A.S. STUND, short space of time.
German STUNDE, hour.

40.—" Lords," L. " earl."
CABBAGE (B. "capage"). In dealing with this word,
which neither Lambe nor Weber have attempted to ex-
plain, we gather from the whole drift of the stanza that
some kind of bedding or covering must be meant. In
the *Whitby Glossary* we find CABAJEEN with the gloss, " a
cloak of eighty years ago," a time which we may define
as " in our forefathers' days." In Morris' *Specimens of
Early English* we find CAPADOS, a hood. We venture
then to surmise that the meaning of cabbage in this
stanza is simply " covering," or " nightcap," which will
be perfectly consonant with the meaning of the rest of
the stanza.

41.—HASTLY (L. " quickly ") = hastily.

43.—" Underlay'd," W. " understood."
Second line, L.—They cannot well be understood.
LEASING = lies. A.S. LEASUNG, falsehood ; LEAS, false.

44.—QUO' = QUOTH, said. This preterite is the only tense re-
maining in use of the A.S. CWETHAN, to say. The verb
to " bequeath " is a compound form of it.
Last two lines, L.—
He did not forge the same nor feign,
Nor do we any favour need.

45.—Second line, L.—Who truly did the same reveal.

46.—MUSE = wonder.

47.—" To the earl," W. " again to him."

48.—" You do make," W. "ye did make ;" L. "you make such."
BIDDETH MUTE = declines to answer.

52.—UNTIL = to, towards. In this signification the preposition
until, now obsolete, generally followed its case, as in this
stanza.

53.—THOROUGH=through, always followed its case ; see preceding gloss.
    SENT = sent to him.
    " He being," L. " to him."

54.—No FAR = nothing further.

55.—" Earl Surrey," W. " the Earl."

56.—" To fight," L. " would fight."
    PLIGHT = plighted.

57.—" Clept," L. " kept, " evidently a misprint.

58.—"When as," L. " when this."

62.—" Inclose," L. " did not lose."
    " With fenny mire," L. " about with mire."
    GRIZZLY = dreadful.
    GILLS = ravines. An Icelandic word, current in all the
    northern counties, though the manner or period of its
    introduction is uncertain. Though absent from the
    modern Danish and Norse, it must have existed in the
    early Scandinavian of which Icelandic is a remnant.
    MOSS = bog.

63.—BAD = bade, bid.

64.—HENT = to catch, to seize A. S. HENTAN.
    W. makes this stanza the first of the seventh fit, and Lambe
    includes the whole of Heron's episode in the sixth fit.

FIT VII.

1.—PREST (W. & L. " press'd ") = ready.
    SCOWRING = galloping.
    LUSTY = strong.

2.—VAILED = lowered.
    RADLY (L. "swiftly") = swiftly A.S. RAD and RÆD,
    active, thence the modern " ready."

3—" Knight," W. " wight," L. " none of them all."

4.—L.— From off his steed he leaped there
      And kneeling, gracefully did bow,
        Holding his horse and quivering spear.
    LOUT = to bend, to stoop. A. S. LUTIAN. Still heard
    occasionally in northern dialects, in the signification
    of " to greet humbly."

5.—L.— In little time he silence brake,
    My lord, quoth he, afford some grace,
    Pardon my life for pity's sake,
    For now you are in King Henry's place.

6.—First line, L.— Mercy, my lord, from you I crave.
    " I may," L. " I shall."

7—" Belike thou'st," L. " Perhaps you have."
    Belike = probably.
    Fact = deed.

9.—Second line, L.— My lord, my crime it is not such.

10.—Last line, L.— And to extreams I have been forced.

11.—" Murth'ring," L. " hurting."

13.—Second line, L.— You seem to be a person brave.
    Prave = bad, from the Latin pravus.

14.—Wight = active, brave.

16.—Sleight = trick.

17.—" Thereto," W. " therefore."   " Heron," W. " Hearon."
    Upbrought = brought up. See gloss to stanza 38, page 98.

19.—Deemed = doomed. A. S. deman, to judge.   The old
    English word dempster, judge, is still in active use in
    the Isle of Man.

20.—To prove = by token.
    " The king," W. & L. " King Henry."

21.—Gate, in all the northern dialects bears the signification
    of " road," " street," not gateway.   The " town gate" in
    the Craven villages is the principal street.
    Wot = know.   A. S. witan, from which our substantive
    " wit."   The preterite form wot was generally used in a
    present signification instead of I weet, much as the Latin
    cognovi.

22.—Unfold = uncover.
    Opened = explained.

23.—Wist (L. " knew"), a second preterite of the verb to weet,
    see gloss to stanza 21, ante.

24.—" Wile " is omitted in L.

27.—Second line, L.—Who, 'fraid of townsmen, careful watched.
    For = in the place of.
    Stead = place.   A. L. stede, German stætte.
    Despatched = hastened.

28.—FRAME = contrive.
  "Soon 't was," W. "as it was," L. "soon as."

29.—MADE BOWN = prepared. L. "soon were bown." The
  adjective BOWN or BOUN, is from the Icelandic participle
  BUINN. The root is the same as in BUSK, for which see
  gloss to stanza 56, page 96.

32.—DOOM = sentence; see ante, gloss to stanza 19.

33.—MANSION, in its original meaning of dwelling-place.
  "Open I appeared," W. "I aptly appeared," L. "openly I
  came."

34.—WEET, see glosses to stanzas 21 & 23, ante.
  STEAD = place.

35.—SAM = together. Old English ALLE-SAMEN, all together :
  Swiss Allemanic, ALLI-ZAMME.
  GAND, which Lambe actually refers to a Spanish card game,
  or to a ball with which the Lapland wizards divert them-
  selves!, is from the Danish verb GANTE, to make a fool
  of, to banter, and therefore means "trick."
  GAM = game, fun. It is still used in the north in the
  same form.
  FAIN = glad, a northern dialect word.
  "Refrain," W. "abstain."
  First line, L.—So said, the lords and knights of fame.

36.—POLICY = national sentiments.
  Lambe inserts here the following stanza, in order to
  terminate the fit :—
      Read the fourth part, it makes an end
        Of Heron's story, and the fight.
      Let young and old to this attend,
        It will give instruction with delight.

37.—This being the first stanza of the fourth part and seventh
  fit in L.'s edition, "he fiercely flew" is altered to "brave
  Heron flew."

39.—"They all," L. "they were."

40.—BODE (L. "stood") = abode, awaited.

43.—WAST = waste.

44.—BLACK = dismal. Compare Shakespeare, Richard III, IV. 4.
  WAN (L. "won") = insipid; pale. A. S. WANA, wanting.

45.—STEADFUL = steadfast.

47.—YERD = yard measure. A. S. GYRD, wand, German GERTE.
  "Fear'd," L. "afraid."

49.—" Scoulding Scots," F. " beaten Scots."

50.—HEALTH = safety.
" Scots do get," L. " Scotsmen gain."

51.—Second line L.— But, cowards-like, from them should turn.
HARRY = to plunder. A. S. HERGIAN.

52.—STICK = Scruple.

53.—" Spoil," W. & L. " soil."
WEILD = have at command.

54.—DRIVE FORTH (L. " pass out ") = live, pass.
" perduring," L. " a lasting."

55.—ALL SAM (L. " agreed ") = all together; see gloss to stanza
35, ante.
BENT = fixed purpose, determination. Lambe's gloss is
" bent, a field," which Weber adopts. Although bent is
met with in Old English in the meaning of " slope of a
hill " (see Morris' Specimens), yet I think the meaning
of " determination," for which see Latham, s. v., suits
the general drift of the stanza better ; for evidently the
soldiers, who were still at Sandiford, were not to abide
there " on that field."   Lambe's derivation from bent-
grass is not worthy of refutation.

FIT   VIII.

2.—" In sight they saw," L. " clearly they saw."

3.—" Sunny side," L. " Surrey-side " !

5.—" Was a guileful," L. " then, a gainful."
GREEK = fellow.

6.—PASSING = exceedingly.

7.—MARCHES (W. " marshes ") = borderlands. A. S. MEARC,
boundary.   Compare also the German MARK, ex. Steier-
mark, Markgraf.

9.—TRAINE = artifice, from the Anglo-Norman TRAVE, to
deceive.

10.—Third line, L.— The Scots there scoured with right good
will.
SCOURE = run.
THERR TILL = thither ; see gloss to stanza 52, page 112.

11.—Last two lines, L.—Whose dusty smoak the light did blind,
That both the armies soon they met.
WRASTLING = whirling, from the A. S. WRÆSTIAN, to writhe, to twist.
BET = beat.

12.—This stanza is omitted by Lambe, probably through inadvertence.
FEAL'D, incorrectly translated by Weber as "defiled," means "obscured, hid." See Carr's Craven Dialect, where the derivation is stated to be from the Icelandic FEL, dark. The derivation from the A. S. FEL, covering, is quite as probable.

13.—"At length," L. "For when the." "Now both the hosts," L. "The armies both."

14.—BATTLES = lines.

15.—GAINSTAND = withstand.
BENT = prepared.

17.—HENT = seize.
RUFFLING = violently.

18.—OUTBRAST = burst out.
LEVELLED = cast.

19.—ARCH = chief.

20.—BRAST = burst.
PIPED A PEAL = played a tune.

21.—HENT = got.
SOUSE = to hurl.

22.—"In ragious claps," L. "in furious rage."
RAGIOUS = roaring.

24.—PREASE (L. "press") = to press forward. "Of his beauteous son I prease to sing," Peele's David and Bethsade (Old MS.).

25.—GROOM = young man.

26.—GREY GOOSE WING. This is a favourite expression, used by our older popular writers to denote the flight of the arrow. We meet with it again in stanza 14 of the ninth fit.
SCOUR = clear away.
SKAIL = disperse, a northern dialect word. See SKALE in Carr's Craven Dialect.

27.—"A wight his," W. "wight men's," L. "to the."
COIL = stir; see Latham, s. v.

29.—Second line, L.— Another through his stomach stricked.
  STICKT = pierced.

30—" Plied apace," L. " then they went."
  PLIED = turned, hastened. I suspect that this signification
  of the verb to ply must be referred for its origin to the
  French PLIER, to fold, to bend.
  APACE = quickly.

31.—BILLS, BOWS = billmen, bowmen.
  MELL = mace.

32.—" Stretcht," W. " straight.
  PREST = pressed.

33.—MACE. This expression is obscure ; it can scarcely be a
  clerical error for " pace." An ordinary rhyme to " was "
  and an alliteration to " pass " is required ; the word
  " mass," standing for a body of troops, will fulfil these
  conditions and supply a proper meaning.

34.—AGAIN = against, a common dialect word.

35.—TOLD = numbered.

37.—SHOCK (W. & L. " shake ") should be SHACK = shake.
  "O barn, thoo shacks ma," = oh child, you upset me.
  (Cumbrian jocular expression.)
  MINISH = depress.
  Third line, L.— Nor ever let the world suppose.

38.—MOULD = earth.

39.—CHEAR = courage.

41.—The rendering of the second line is :—Who were present
  and eye witnesses.

42.—" Caught," L. " wrought." " Stagger," W. " stacker," the
  latter being the older form, from the A.S. STAKERE, to
  stagger. "Groom," L. " man."
  STOUND = moment.

43.—THRASHING (L. & W. " threshing ") = striking.
  TURNED TO TEENE = brought to grief.

44.—" Slaughtering," L. " slaughter."

45.—" Sever'd," L. " covered."
  SKAILED = dispersed, see gloss to stanza 26, ante.
  ALL SAM, see gloss to stanza 35, page 115.
  " Hash," W. " dash," L. " clash." Alliteration to " his
  helmet high," as well as the sense of the phrase, requires
  hash = hack, from the French HACHER.

47.—" Fierce in," L. " in the."

48.—" Flick'ring," L. " fluttering."
    L. inserts here the following stanza :—
        Who now, entombed, lies at a church
          Carved out in stone to shew his fate,
        That though, by fate, left in the lurch,
          He died a death renowned and great.

49.—WRACK = ruin.

50.—HYED = hastened.

51.—SCOT-FREE. A capital pun, legitimately used. The ordinary
"scot-free" is by Latham derived from the A. S. SCEAT,
payment, though it is questionable whether the derivation
from the Celtic SCOT, contribution, share, is not the more
natural, and more in consonance with its specific meaning.
Compare the French ECOT, derived by French lexico-
graphers from SCOT.

52.—DIGHT = doomed ; see gloss to stanza 33, page 103.

53.—" They flung," W. " lay flung."
    UPDREW = rose.

55.—Fourth line, L.— Two Scotch earls of an ancient race.

57.—SALLETS (L. "solid") = headpiece, helmet, from the
    French SALADE.
    RIVEN = torn.

59.—" Foes," W. " enemies "; alliteration demands " foes."
" Person," L. " battle "; alliteration demands " person."
PREST = ready.
BLAZED = waving.

60.—" Wherein," L. " under which."

63.—SUM = number.

64.—" Captains great and," W. " the captains of."
    ADDREST = directed.

65.—KEEN = brave.

66.—Last three lines L.—
        And blows with cutting axes dealt,
        Then towering helmets through were cut.
         That some their wounds scarce ever felt.
    SWAP = blow. A. S. SWAPAN, to strike.
    SWELT = faint. A. S. SWELTAN, to die.

67.—This stanza is not given by Lambe.
    SOUN = swoon, northern dialect word.
    RAGEOUSLY = violently.

68.—This stanza is not given by W.

FIT IX.

1.—Fourth line, L.— Unto the English fierce did thrust.
    THRAST = push, penetrate.

2.—Last line, L.— A valiant Englishman him slew.

3.—"Hardy," S. "haughty."   "Fine," L. "end."
    FINE = end.

4.—"Weet might," L. "could say."
    WEET = know.
    W. & L. terminate the eighth fit here, although in the
    midst of a sentence.

5.—FAST = fasten, cause to adhere.
    "Foot," W., L. & F. "feet,"

6.—First line, W.—And some their boots left down below.
    Third line, W.— Some from their feet the shoes did throw.
    "Toes," L. "loose it."   "Throw," L. "thraw," the latter
    being the true northern form.

7.—WAN = gained.
    WIST = knew, preterite of TO WEET.

8.—"All sam," L. "at last."
    HARDY = bold, in the signification of the French HARDI.

9—Last two lines, L.— With fighting fierce, much fear have I,
                 Lest that they should be overlaid.

    "They be," W "may be."
    FEAR ME. This verb is not unfrequently used as a pro-
    nominal verb by our older writers, a usage productive
    of great force and elegance.
    OVERLAID = overborne.

11.—Last line, L.— Stanley will be to you a guide.

12.—BARWICK = Berwick.

13.—BESETS = presses.

14.—"Anon," F. "arrows."   "Amongst," W. "against."
"flickering," L. "fluttering.',
GREY GOOSE WING = arrow's flight.

16.—This stanza is not given by Lambe.
PAVISH = buckler, from the French PAVOIS which is itself
derived from the Italian PAVESE, small square shield of
wood, covered over with strips of leather, and worn on
the left arm.

16.—FRAME = set about; West Riding provincialism.
Last line, L.— A narrow dint of dangerous bode.
Weber inserts here the following stanza:—
And when the shower of arrows shot,
Did somewhat cease within awhile ;
The earl of Huntley haughty and hot,
With the earl of Lenox and Argile,

17.—Last two lines L.—
Endured death through danger's force,
Alas ! for them, they staid too long.

18.—THRAST (L, "thrust") = thrust himself.
Last two lines, L.—
My Lancashire brave lads, quoth he,
Down with the Scots this day we must.
"This when the," L. "which when lord."
WAST = waste.

19.—EARL, as explained in gloss to stanza 25, page 90, is a
dissyllable ; Lambe, unaware of it, altered the expression
to "the Scots earl."

20.—Lenox' luck was," L. "Lenox luck had."
BENT = field ; see gloss to stanza 55, page 116.

21.—HAP = luck.

24.—SCOURING = galloping.
SCAPT = escaped.
"But he by hap had," L. "for having near a."

25.—"Dead or," W. "fallen and." The former is a correct
rhyme, the latter a correct alliteration to " fled."

Last two lines, L—
Their soldiers then did fly with speed ;
With souls of horror and distress.

24.—LIGHT = came upon.

MAIN = might.

Second Line, L.— Swiftly pursues unto the plain.

26.—First line, W.— But when the English arrows shot.

OUTBROKE (L. " were shot ") = burst forth.

27.—" Hardly he could," L. " he could scarce." " Fight any more," F. " see his foes."

LIGHT = struck him (alighted on).

BLEMISHED = obscured.

28.—This stanza is not given by Lambe.

" Stay'd," F. " said"

31.—This stanza appears in the Fragments in the midst between the two preceding stanzas.

DEVICE = intelligence, mind.

FAILED = sunk, fainted. Had not all the mss. and editions concurred in giving " fail'd," I should have suspected that " fell " was intended.

32.—IN BASE BEGOT = bastard.

33.—First line, W.— As the earl of Catness and Castel.

" Athell," L. " Atholl."

34.—" Hands none," W. " fact few," " Was brought," L. & F. " gave way." " Was thought," L. & F. " was he."

35.—" To ground," W. " to flight." " Till sun went down," W. " while sun gave light."

COMMONS = rank and file.

37.—COSTLY = opulent.

38.—This stanza appears neither in L. nor F.

UNCASED = stripped.

'RAY = outfit, array.

39.—" Born," L. & F. " found." " So well," L. " right," F. " aright." " Morn," L. & F. " ground."

40.—Last three lines, L. & F.,—

        By certain signs did know the king ;

        His corps into a cart being placed

        They to Newcastle did it bring.

Bewray = identify. This verb is essentially different from BETRAY, being derived from the A.S. BEWREGAN, to show truly, allied to the German WAHR and the Latin VERUS, whereas the root of " betray," must be sought in the French TRAHIR, from the Latin TRADERE.

41.—Instead of this and the following three stanzas (the last in this and W's. edition) Gent, Lambe, and the Fragments have these five :—

> Twelve thousand Scots it seems were slain,
>   Of English but five thousand fell ;
> But fifteen hundred, others plain
>   As words can make it to us tell.
> Great store of guns were likewise taken,
>   Amongst the rest seven culverines ;
> Seven sisters called, which do remain,
>   To be talked of to latest times.
> King James's body was embalmed,
>   Sweet, like a king, and then was sent
> To Shene in Surrey, where entombed,
>   Some say there is now a monument.
> But Bryan Tunstall, that brave knight,
>   A never dying honour gains,
> And will as long as day or night,
>   Or as this little book remains.
> Thus have you heard of Flodden fight,
>   Worthy of each to be commended :
> Because that then Old England's right
>   Was bravely by her sons defended.

44.—"Three hundred" should evidently be "five hundred."

HISTORICAL

AND

𝕭iographical 𝕹otes.

THE BATTLE OF FLODDON FIELD,
OR BRANXTON MOOR.

THE battle of Floddon was fought on the 9th September, 1513, in the fifth year of the reign of Henry VIII. The events which led up to it are briefly the following.:—On the 24th January, 1502, a perpetual peace had been concluded between James IV. of Scotland and Henry VII. of England, which was further cemented in 1503 by the Scots King marrying Margaret, daughter of Henry VII. This peace did not succeed, however, in putting an end to border raids and mutual bickerings and jealousies, especially when the prudent and pacific Henry VII. was succeeded on the throne of England, in 1509, by his hotheaded and self-willed son Henry VIII., so that it only required a favourable opportunity to fan the glowing embers of national antipathy again into the blaze of overt war. This opportunity was afforded in 1513, by the absence in France of Henry VIII. during his war against Louis XII. Whilst Henry was personally superintending the siege of Thérouanne, near St. Omer in Artois, the Scots king summoned the whole array of his kingdom to assemble on the borough moor of Edinburgh, alleging the ancient alliance between Scotland and France and various grievances relating to the dowry of Margaret, as pretexts for invading England. It is stated that nearly 100,000 men answered the summons of their sovereign, and with this formidable array James IV. crossed the border, west of Berwick which was at that time strongly held by the English, on the 22nd August, 1513, taking after a short resistance the castles of Norham and Ford. Instead, however, of pushing through the almost defenceless northern marches into the heart of the kingdom, James tarried in the neighbourhood of the Tweed, irresolute what course to take.

The result of this indecision might have been foreseen: great numbers of the fickle highlanders, always disinclined to fight in distant expeditions, returned to their homes, and the Scottish army in less than a fortnight, dwindled down to little more than half its original number of men. This delay, on the other hand, enabled the earl of Surrey, lieutenant-general of the northern marches, to collect his forces near Alnwick and oppose the invader with an army of about 30,000 men.

On the 6th September, 1513, the Scots fixed their headquarters on Floddon hill, the extreme north-eastern spur of the Cheviot range. On that day James IV. received and accepted a formal challenge from the earl of Surrey, for the two armies to engage in pitched battle on Friday, the 9th September. During the intermediate time, the earl of Surrey, advancing from Bolton-in-Glendale in a north-easterly direction, crossed the river Till, the southern affluent of the Tweed, and by this bold and skilful flank march cut the Scots off from their base. It is difficult to understand why the Scots made no attempt to impede this turning movement: some writers, chiefly Scottish, attribute it to the exaggerated notions of chivalry entertained by James IV.; others, with more probability, to the divided counsels of the Scottish leaders and to the utter absence of efficient organization in the host under their command.

On Thursday evening, 8th September, the two armies faced each other, ranged in line of battle, and at dawn on Friday the fight commenced with an intermittent artillery fire, which was kept up on both sides, without much effect, till after noon. The first actual onslaught was made by the Scottish left, led by the earls of Huntley and Home, upon the right wing of the English army, commanded by lord Edmond Howard, youngest son of the commander-in-chief. This attack was pushed home so vigourously, that the English ranks became broken and the safety of the whole army would have been seriously compromised, if the highlanders had pursued their advantage instead of giving way to their inveterate habit of pillaging. This fatal mistake, however, enabled lord Dacres to hasten to the assistance of lord Howard, rally the broken English ranks, and overwhelm the disordered host of Scottish plunderers.

The extreme English left, commanded by Sir Edward Stanley, was faced by the Scottish right wing which consisted of clansmen of Lennox and Argyle under their hereditary chiefs. These highlanders, galled by the accurate practice of the English bowmen, prematurely made a furious but ill-regulated attack, which was firmly withstood by the close English ranks and converted into a disorderly flight.

Meanwhile the fight raged with the greatest fury between the two centres, James having left his safe position on the hill in order to relieve the two wings by a central attack on which he staked the fate of his army. But practised discipline prevailed over impulsive valour, and the battle which lasted till after sundown, resulted in the death of the Scottisn King and nearly 10,000 of his subjects,—the most terrible defeat ever inflicted upon Scotland and one which crippled its resources for generations afterwards.

The day after the battle, the body of king James was found among the slain, covered with wounds inflicted by sword and by arrows : the neck was opened to the middle, and the left hand almost cut off, so that it scarcely clung to the arm. A great number of noblemen lay dead round the king, for at a critical moment of the battle they had clustered round their sovereign, so that all the leading men shared his tragic fate, including twelve earls and the archbishop of St. Andrews ; Sir William Scott and Sir John Foreman were the only ones of his personal attendants who escaped with their lives. The royal corpse was carried to York and kept there until king Henry's return from France, when it was taken to Richmond to be gazed at by that monarch.

CONTEMPORARY ACCOUNT OF THE BATTLE.

The earliest authentic account we have of the battle of Floddon and the transactions in immediate connection with it, is a black letter tract printed by Richard Fawkes of St. Paul's Church Yard, London. This printer, who flourished from 1509 to 1530, is stated by Dibdin, on the authority of Ames, to have been the second son of John Fawkes, of Farnley Hall, in Yorkshire. The tract in question was reprinted in facsimile in 1822, at Newcastle, by William Garret, and we proceedto give it in extenso:—

¶ Hereafter ensue the trewe encountre or Batayle lately don betwene Englande and Scotlande. In whiche batayle the Scottsshe Kynge was slayne.

¶ The maner of th' auduaucesynge of my lord of Surrey tresourier and Marshall of Englande and leuetennte generall

of the north pties of the same with xxvi. M. men to wardes the
kynge of Scott. and his Armye vewed and nombred to an hundred
thousande men at the leest.

Firste my sayd Lorde at his beynge at Awnewick in North-
umbrelande the iiij. daye of Septembre the v. yere of ye Reygne
of kynge Henry the viij. herynge that ye kynge of Scottes thenne
was removed from Norhme And dyd lye at forde Castel & in those
ptyes dyd moche hurte in spoylyng robynge and brennynge sent
to the sayde kynge of Scottes Ruge Cros purseuaunte at Armes
to shewe unto hym that for so moche as he the sayd kynge contrary to his honour all good reason & conscyence And his oothe
of Fidelite for ye ferme entartnynge of perpetuall peas betwene
the kyng hygnes our Souerayne lorde and hym had inuaded this
Raalme spoylad brente and robbyd dyuers and sondery townes
and places in the same. Also had caste and betten downe the
Castel of Norhme And crewella had murdered & slayne many
of the kynges liege people he was comen to gyue hym bayta.
And desyred hym yt for so moche as he was a kynge and a great
Prynce he wolde of his lusty & noble courage cosent therunto
and tarrye ye same. And for my sayde Lordes partie his lordeshyp
promysed ye assured Accomplysshement and perfourmaunce
thereof as he was true knyght to god and the kynge his mayster.
The kynge of Scottes herynge this message reynued & kep to wt
hym ye sayd Ruge Cros purseuante & wolde nat suffre hym at
ye tyme to retourne agayne to my sayd lorde. The v. daye of
of Septembre his lordshyp in hys approchynge nyghe' to the
borders of Scotlande mustred at Bolton in glendayll & lodged
that nyght therein yt felde with all his Armye.

¶ The nexte daye beynge the vi daye of Septembre the kynge
of scottes sent to my sayd lorde of Surrey a harolde of his called
Ilaye and demaunded if that my sayde Lorde wolde iustefye the
message sent by the sayd purseuaunte ruge cros as is aforesayd
sygnefyinge that if my lorde wolde so doo it was the thynge that
moost was to his Joye and comforte. To this demaunde my
lord made answere afore dyuers lordes knyghtes and gentylme
nyghe iij myles from the felde where ys the sayde harolde was
apstoynted to tarye bycause he shulde nat vewe the Armye
that he commaunded nat oonly the sayde Ruge-cros to speke and
shewe the seyde werdes of his message But also gaue and com-
ytted unto hym the same by Instruccyon sygned and subscrybed
with his owne hande whiche my sayde lorde sayd he wolde
Justefye and for so moche as his lordshyp conceyued by the
sayde Harolde how Joyous and comfortable his message was to

ye sayde kynge of scottes he therefore for the more assuraunce
of his message shewed that he wolde be bounden in x Mli &
good suertes with his Lordshyp to gyve the sayde kynge batayle
by Frydaye next after at the furthest If that the sayde kynge
of scottes wolde assyne and appoynte any other Erle or Erles
of his Realme to be bounden in lyke maner that he wolde abyde
my sayde lordes commynge And for so moche as the sayd kynge
of Scottes reynued styll with him Ruge Cros purseuaunte and
wolde nat suffre hym to retourne to my lorde my sayde lorde in
lyke & semblable maner dyd kepe with hym the scottesshe
Harolde Ilay and sant to the sayd kynge of scottes with his
answere and further offer as is afdre rehersed A gentylman
of scotlande that accompanyed and came to my sayde lorde with
sayd Harolde Ilay And thus Ilay contynved and was kepte close
tyll the commynge home of Ruge Cros whiche was the next daye
after And thenne Ilay was put at large and lyberte to retourne
to the kynge of scottes his maystere to shewe my lordes answres
declaracyons and goodly offers as he had hade in euery be haluc
of my sayde lorde.

¶ The same daye my Lorde deuyded his Arme in two betaylles
that is to wytte in a vaunwarde and a rerewarde and ordeyned
my lord Hawarde Admorall his son to be Capitayne of the sayde
vaunwarde and hymselfe to be chefe Capitayne of the rerewarde.

¶ In the breste of ye sayde vaunwarde was wt the sayde Lorde
Admorall ix thousande men and vnder Capitaynes of the same
breste of the batayle was the lord Lumley = syr Willm Bulmer
= the baron of Hylton and dyverse other of the Bysshopryche
Duresme = vnder Seynt = Cuthbert banner the lorde Scrope
of vpsall the lorde Ogle syr wyllyam Gascoygne ser Cristofer
warde syr John Eueringhm sir walter Griffith syr John Gower
and dyvers other Esquyres and gentylmen of yorkeshyre and
Northumberland And in ayther wynge of the same batayle was
iij M. men.

¶ The Capitayne of the right wynge was mayster Edmonde
hawarde sone to my seyde lorde of Surrey And with hym was syr
Thomas Butler syr John Boothe syr Richard Boolde and dyuerse
other Esquyres & gentylmen of Lancasshyre and Chasshyre.

¶ The Capitayne of the last wynge was olda syr Marmaduke
Constable & with hym was mayster wyllm Percy his sona Elawe
willm Constable his broder syr Robert Constable marmaduke
Constable willm Constable his sones And syr John Constable
of holdernes with dyuerse his kynesmen Allies and other
gentylmen of yorkeshyre and Northumberlande.

¶ In the breste of the batayle of the sayde rerewarde was v M. men with my sayde lorde of Surrey and vnder Capitaynes of the same was the lord Scrope of Bolton syr Philype Tyney broder Elawe to my sayd lord of Surrey George darcy sone and heyre to the lorde Darcy sayde beynge Capitayne of the firste batayle of the Scottes fyersly dyd sette vpon maister Edmonde Hawarde Capitayne of the vttermoste parte of the felde at the west syde And betwene them was so cruell batayle that many of our partie Chesshyremen and other dyd flee And the sayd mayster Edmonde in maner lefte alone without socoure and his standerde and berer of the same beten and hewed in peces and hymsel thryse stryken downe to the ground Howbeit lyke a couragyous & an hardy yonge lusty gentylman he recouered agayne and faught hande to hande with one sir Dauy home & slewe hym with his owne handes. And thus the sayde mayster Edmonde was in great perell and daunger tyll that the lorde Dacre lyke a good and an hardy knyght releued and came vnto hym for his socoure.

¶ The seconde Batayle came vpon my lorde Hawarde The thirde batayle wherin was the kynge of Scottes & moste parte of the noble men of his Reame came fyersly vpon my sayd lord of Surrey whiche two bataylles by the helpe of elmyghty god were after a greht confydelycte venquysshed ouercomen betten downe & put to flyght and fewe of them escaped with theyr lyves syr Edwarde Stanley beynge at the vttermoste parte of the sayde rerewarde one heste partie seynge the fourthe batayle redy to releue the sayde kynge of scottes batayle couragyously and lyke a lusty and an hardy knyght dyd sette vpon the same and ouercame & put to flyght all the scottes in the sayd batayle. And thus by the grace socour and helpe of almyghty god victory was gyven to the Reame of England And all the scottyshe ordenance wonne & brought to Ettell and Barwyke in Suretie.

¶ Hereafter ensueth the names of sondry noblemen of the scottes slayne at the sayde batayle & felde called Brainston moore.

> Firste ye kyng of scottes.
> The Archebysshop of seynt Androwes.
> The bysshop of Thyles.
> The bysshop of Ketnes.
> The abbot ynchaffrey.
> The abbot of Rylwenny.
> Therle of Mountroos.
> Therle of Craforde.
> Therle of Argyle.
> Therle of lennox.

Therle of Lencar
Therle of Castelles.
Therle of Boothwell.
Therle Arell. Constable
Lorde Lowett.
Lorde Forboos.
Lorde Elweston.
Lorde Inderby.
Lorde Maxwell.
Mac Keyn.
Mac Cleen.
John of graunte.
The maist. of Agwis.
Lorde Roos.
Lorde tempyll.
Lorde Borthyke.
Borde Askyll.
Lorde Dawisfye.
Sir Alexander Scotton.
Sir John home.
Lord Coluin.
Sir Dauy home.
Cuthbert home of Fascastell.

Over & above the seyd psones there at slayne of the Scottes
vewd by my lorde Dacre the noumbre of xi or xii thousande
mend And of Englysshmen slayne & taken prysoners vpon xii C.
dyuers prysoners are taken of ye scottes But noo Notable person
saue oonly syr wyllm Scotte knyght Councellour of the sayde
kynge of scottes and as is sayd a gentylman well lerned Also sr
John Forma knyght broder to the Bysshop of Murrey which
bysshop as is reported was & is moost pryncypall procurour
of this warre And one other called sr John Colehome many
other scottysshe prysoner coude and myght haue been taken but
they were soo vengeable & cruell in their fyghtynge that whenne
Englysshmen had the better of them they wolde nat saue them
though it so were that dyuerse scottes offered great sumes
of money for theyr lyues.

¶ It is to be noted that the felde beganne betwcen iiij and v
at after Noone and contynued within nyght if it had fortuned to
haue ben further afore nyght many mo scottes had ben slayne
and taken prysoners louyinge beto almyghty god all the noble
men of Englande tha were vpon the same felde bothe lordes and
knyghtes are safe from any hurte And none of theym awantynge
saue oonly maister Harrgy Gray syr Huinfeide lyle bothe pryson-

ers in Scotlade syr John Gower of Yorkesshyre and syr John Boothe of Lancasshyre both wantynge and as yet not founden.

¶ In this batayle the scottes hade many great Auauntagies that is to wytte the hyghe Hylles and mountaynes a great wynde with them and sodayne rayne all contrary to our bowes and Archers.

¶ It is nat to be doubted but the scottes fought manly and were determyned outher to wynne ye Felde or to dye They were also as well apoynted as was possyble at all poyntes with Armoure & harneys so that fewe of them were slayne with arrowes Howbeit the bylles did bete and hewe them downe woth some payne and daunger to Englysshemen.

The sayd scottes were so playnely determyned to abyde batayle and nat to flee that they put from them theyr horses and also put of theyr botes and shoes and faught in the vampis of theyr hooses every man for the moost ptie with a kene and a shape spere of v yerdes longe and a target aforh hym And when theyr speres fayled and wera spent then they faught with great end sharpe swerdes makyng lyttell or no noys vithoue that ; that for the ptie many of them wolde desyre to be saued.

¶ The felde where ye scottes dyd lodge was nat to be reprouyd but rather to be comended greatly for there many and great nombre of goodiyl tenttes and moche good stuffe in the same & in the sayd felde was plentie of wyne bere ale beif mutton salfysshe chese and other vytalles necessary and conuenyent for suche a great Army Albeit our Armye doutynge that the sayd vyttalyes hadde ben poysoned for theyr distruccyon wolde nat saue but vtterly distroyed theym.

¶ Hereafter ensueth the names of suche noble men as after the Felde were made knyght for theyr valyauce Act in the same by my sayd lorde therle of Surrey.

> ¶ Firste my lord Scrope of vpsall.
> Sir willm Percy.
> Sir Edmonde Hawarde.
> Sir george Darcy.
> Sir w. gascoygne ye yoger.
> Sir willm. Medlton.
> Sir willm. Maleuerdy.
> Sir Thomas Bartley.
> Sir marmaduke Costable ye yoger.
> Sir xpofer Dacre.
> Sir John Hoothome.

Sir Nicholas Appleyarde.
Sir Edwarde Goorge.
Sir Rauf Ellercar the yoger.
Sir John wylivby.
Sir Edwarde Echinghme.
Sir Edwarde Musgraue.
Sir John stanley.
Sir Walter stonner.
Sir Nyniane martynfelde.
Sir Raffe Bowes.
Sir Briane stapleton of wyghall.
Sir Guy Dawny.
Sir Raffe salwayne.
Sir Richarde Malleuerey.
Sir willm. Constable of Hatefelde.
Sir willm. Constable of Larethorpe.
Sir Xpofer Danby.
Sir Thomas Burght.
Sir willm. Rous.
Sir Thomas Newton.
Sir Roger of Fenwyke.
Sir Roger Gray.
Sir Thomas Connyers.
My lorde Ogle.
Sir Thomas strngewase.
Sir Henri Thiuaittes.
My lorde lumley.
Sir Xpofe Pekerynge.
Sir John Bulmer.

¶ Emprynted by me Richarde Faques dwllyng In poulys churche yerde.

THE AUTHORSHIP AND VARIOUS EDITIONS OF THE BALLAD.

The authorship of this historical ballad is involved in obscurity. The supposition of Lambe, that it was written by "a schoolmaster of Yorkshire," has great probability in its favour, for the occurrence in the poem of a considerable number of dialect words appertaining exclusively to the Craven district in the West Riding of Yorkshire, and the absence of purely Northumbrian

words, tend to corroborate the tradition that the ballad was
originally written by one "Richard Jackson," a schoolmaster
of Ingleton (in the very centre of Craven), about fifty years after
the battle. This would fix the date of its composition approxi-
mately between the years 1560 and 1570. Weber, who does not
appear to have been aware of the supposed authorship of Richard
Jackson and the "fifty years after the battle" date given with it,
arrives curiously enough at the same result from internal evidence. We quote his words:—

"We are entirely in the dark respecting the time in which our
Minstrel flourished. The date of the only ancient MS. which at
present is to be found, is about 1636, as will immediately be
shewn. There can, however, be little doubt, that it was produced during the preceding century. After the accession of James
to the throne of England, the battle would not have been the
subject of popular celebration. A remarkable instance of the
deference paid to this monarch on this score, occurs in the history of the Mirrour of Magistrates. Two poems on the subject
of Floddon Field and the death of James IV., which had been
introduced into the edition of 1587, and which, in point of merit,
are certainly not inferior to the generality of the legends in that
collection, were omitted in the edition of 1610.

"The deviations which occur in the poem, from those popular
historians, Hall and Holinshed, and which would probably not
have occurred, had the author been acquainted with their Chronicles, might lead us to assign a much earlier date to it. One of
the most interesting incidents is not at all noticed by either of
them ; nor have I been able to meet with it in any other chron-
icler of the time. The author must therefore have had some other
sources of information ; most probably traditions in the house
of Stanley, to which he seems to have been attached. The very
frequent and obvious alliteration, is another and a very strong
proof of the antiquity of the work. From all these deductions,
the assertion that it was produced about the middle of the 16th
century will not be deemed rash."

"The great and strongly-marked partiality for the house of
Stanley, and the Lancastrian forces, and the more minute detail
of their operations, indicate a close connection of the *maker* with
that family. That this was not his only production, is proved
by the first stanza of the poem, where he very evidently alludes
to another, in which he had celebrated King Henry VIII.'s feats
before Therouenne and Tournay. Ballad-inditing was probably
his principal, if not his sole occupation."

The earliest existing manuscript (i.e. transcript) of the Ballad
is in the British Museum (Harl. MSS. No. 3526), and has the
following title :—" Heare is the famous historie or songe, called
Floodan Field ; in it shalbe declare how, whyle Kinge Henrie the
Eight was in France, the King of Scoots, called James, the fowerth
of that name, invaded the realme of England ; and how he was
incountred with all at a place called Branton, on Floodan Hill,
by the Earl of Surry, liuetenant-generall for the kinge, with the
helpe of dyvers lords and knights in the North Countrie, as the
Lord Dakers of the North, the Lord Scrope of Bolton, with the
most coragious knight Sir Edward Standley, who for his prowis
and valliantnes, shewed att the said battell, was made Lord
Mount Eagle, as the sequel declareth."—The date of this MS.
is about A.D. 1636.

The first printed edition appeared in 1664, as a 12mo volume,
under the following title :—" Floddan Field, in Nine Fits, being
an exact History of that famous memorable Battle, fought
between English and Scots on Floddan Hill, in the time of Henry
the Eighth, anno 1513: worthy the perusal of the English Nobility.   London, printed by P. L. for H. B., W. P. and S. H. and
are to be sold in Ivy-Lane and Gray's-inn-gate, 1664.   Licensed
November 11th, 1663.   Roger L'Estrange."—Weber took this
copy, then in the possession of Sir Walter Scott, as the text
of his excellent edition.

Another printed edition, taken, however, from a different
source, viz., the manuscript in the possession of John Askew,
Esq., of Palinsburn, in the county of Northumberland, was issued
by the celebrated printer Thomas Gent, of York, and furnishes
the text to the present edition.   It is undated, but from internal
evidence must be placed between the years 1755 and 1762.   We
learn from Davis' exhaustive " Memoirs of the York Press," that
Gent no longer possessed a printing press in 1772, and that the
last productions of his press, subsequent to 1762, were wretch-
edly printed on vile paper, the failing strength and absolute
poverty of the broken down old man disabling him from turning
out any creditable work.   The last work of any pretension published by Gent, was the second edition of his History of the
East Window in York Cathedral, which appeared in 1762 and
already showed in its paper and type his straitened circumstances.   The " Battle of Floddon," on the other hand, is a
specimen of Gent's best style : the type is handsome and must
have been new or nearly new when used to print that volume ;
the paper is of tolerable quality, superior to that of all his later

works. We can, therefore, scarcely err in ascribing to Gent's "Floddon" an earlier date than to the second edition of his "East Window." It is not likely, on the other hand, to have been printed previous to 1755, for up to that date his volumes contain numerous references to his other works, whilst no allusion to "Floddon" is found in any of them.

The title is as follows :—" The Famous Old Ballad or History of the Battles of Floddon Field. Which were fought between the English under the Earl of Surrey, (in the absence of King Henry VIII. of England, who was fighting in France) and the Scots under their valiant King James IVth of Scotland, who was slain in the said Battle, in the Year of our Blessed Lord, 1513. Containing the valiant and renowned Actions of several Lords, Knights and 'Squires. Part I. York: Printed by Thomas Gent."

" To the Gentlemen, Yeomen, and Others, on the Borders of Yorkshire, and the Borders and Fells of Lancashire, this Poem of Floddon-Field is most humbly Dedicated."

Followed by the argument :—

"Whilst King Henry the VIIIth of England was employ'd in his war against France, James the IVth, King of Scotland, invaded England in Person, with an Army of Fifty Thousand Men; and, after a few days Siege, took Norham Castle. Upon which, Thomas Earl of Surrey, with his eldest Son Lord Admiral Howard, and brave Sir Edward Stanley, having an Army of Twenty Six Thousand Men, march'd towards King James, who had remov'd to a Hill, call'd Floddon, and sent the King a Challenge by the Herald at Arms. The last battle began, after Provocations given, and Speeches made to encourage the soldiers on either side ; and then the King's Battallion and the Earl's maintain'd a long and cruel Fight. But the Earl's youngest Son Sir Edmund Howard was at first distresst, by the valour of the Earls of Lenox and Argyle ; when the Lord Dacres coming to his Succour, as also one Heron, the fight was renew'd with great vigour. In the mean time, Sir Edward Stanley, by Means of his Archers, constrain'd the Scots to descend the Hills; whose distress, perceived by King James, he performed wonders in his Person; but pressing forward, he valiantly dy'd in the Field of Battle. His Body was after honourably interr'd in Shene in Surrey, haing reyn'd Twenty Five Years and was in the Thirty Ninth of his Age. The Scots being defeated, lost most of their Nobility, one Arch-Bishop, Two Bishops, 4 Abbots, and Ten Thousand others ; and on the English side Five Thousand. King Henry returning to England, made the Earl of Surrey

Duke of Northumberland, his eldest Son Lord Thomas Howard Earl of Surrey, and Sir Edward Stanley Lord Mount-eagle, for their brave Achievements in Floddon Field."

To part II. the following note is prefixed :—" In the first Part of these Battles, it was very hard to make out the Copy, it being much obliterated, and the leaves worn out in many places, so that some words were forc'd to be added, and others more obsolete changed for the Ease of the Readers. How far it may give Content they alone are to be Judges.   Indeed the Poem itself seems little inferior to that written on the famous Battle of Chevy-Chase, which yet has not that lovely Description of the pleasant Vallies, Mountains and Rivers, (so well known in the Country) as this contains.   Homer and Virgil are indeed more rofin'd ; but one may venture to say, has not more Nature and Truth in their Poems. No false Gods are usher'd in to the Assistance of the English Heroes, but the true Almighty invok'd by the Prayers of the Church and People.   And as this Poem is redeemed from the Jaws of Time a while longer, methinks, at least 'tis hop'd, it will not fail meeting with that Encouragement due to such a painful Undertaking, as being both fit to inform the elder Sort, and to entice Children to their Reading and Learning."

Respecting the merits (or demerits) of Gent's editions, it suffices to say that Gent dealt very summarily with any obscure passages or words in the manuscript before him, by simply omitting them and substituting for them his own lucubrations which in no single instance come up to the rugged and simple beauty of the original text. It has been the care of the editor of the present edition, to restore the original readings of the manuscript, and he has for that purpose collated all the extant authorities, especially the Palinsburn copy.

A third edition of the Ballad was published in 1773 at Berwick, by Robert Lambe, vicar of Norham upon Tweed, which edition was reprinted without alteration in " Ancient Historic Ballads," published at Newcastle in 1807. Weber, in criticizing this edition, did Lambe the honour of seriously refuting his supposed claims to careful editorship, not being aware that Lambe had not even the merit of bringing before the public a bona-fide edition of his own ; for this so-called " edition " is solely a word-for-word reprint of Gent's book which had appeared about twelve years before but had probably only become known to a very limited circle of readers in and about York. Every one of Gent's interpolations, every one of his absurdities is faithfully reproduced by Lambe who, it is evident, simply put Gent's volume as copy into his own printer's hands. It is true that he added an appendix of notes, which add little, however, to the value of the work, for they are prolix and irrelevant where the meaning of the text is perfectly clear, and scanty or entirely absent where a text really requires elucidation. His deficient philological knowledge, moreover, betrayed him into many absurd statements.

A fourth edition, in small 12mo, was published the following year, 1774, by Joseph Benson, "Philomath," and stated to be "collected from ancient manuscripts." Benson appears to have had access to some MS. not now known, for his readings of the text differ in many places essentially both from the 1664 edition and from the Palinsburn copy.

The next occasion on which the "Battle of Floddon" appeared before the public, was in the excellent edition of Henry Weber, which was printed by Ballantyne & Co., Edinburgh, in 1808. It is a handsome 8vo. volume, of 389 pp., illustrated with three plates, and contains, besides the text from the MS. in Sir Walter Scott's possession, a list of various readings, a small glossary, and reprints of several pieces, in prose and verse, which treat of the battle of Floddon. Had not this work become scarce, the editor of the present edition would not have presumed to tread in the steps of so consummate an antiquary as Henry Weber.

A fragmentary edition, small 8vo. 16 pp., undated, was printed at Skipton about the year 1867, but contains only the enumeration of the English forces and the actual fight at Floddon, altogether seventy stanzas. Fragmentary as it is, this little pamphlet is valuable as giving a faithful copy of an early transcript of the Palinsburn MS. We have found its aid invaluable in restoring the text where Gent had "improved" it.

Respecting the merits of the ballad itself, the editor may be permitted to quote Weber's estimate :—

It would be in vain to contend for any great share of poetical merit in the execution ; but the unadorned and faithful manner in which the battle is narrated, and the minute detail given of circumstances, either but slightly touched upon by historians, or utterly unnoticed by them, sufficiently account for the interest excited by it. And though the general conduct of the poem be prolix, and the style too much that of the chronicle ballad writers, who preceded the more polished, but also more dull tragedies of the Mirrour of Magistrates, there are not wanting passages which evince considerable vigour of versification, and spirit of narration; and are certain indications of the abilities of the anonymous author, to have composed a poem of greater merit in point of execution. His object was certainly not posthumous reputation; but to procure his fellow-countrymen of the North of England, particularly those attached like him to the noble house of Stanley, an accurate and minute account of a victory, in which they had gained so much renown."

We may add that no finer specimen of alliterative poetry is to be met with in our early ballad literature.

3.—HENRY VIII., second son of Henry VII. and Elizabeth of York, was born 28 June, 1491. His elder brother Arthur dying without issue in 1502, Henry became heir apparent to the throne, which he actually ascended in 1509. The French wars alluded to in the opening lines of our Ballad, refer in the first instance to the English expedition which was sent in 1512 to the Peninsula, in order to co-operate with Ferdinand V. of Aragon in a proposed invasion of France, which was to bring about the re-conquest of the formerly English province of Gascony. Ferdinand, however, found it more advantageous to make use of his allies for the purpose of adding Navarre to his own possessions, so that the English expedition returned at last to England without having actually set foot on French soil. A fresh expedition which set out the following year, 1513, under the command of the king himself, was however more successful. Henry had entered at the beginning of the year into an alliance (the League of Malines) with the emperor Maximilian, the king of Aragon, and pope Leo X., and to carry out its objects landed in Artois, where he gained the battle of Guinegate, or Battle of Spurs as it is sometimes called, in which the French gendarmerie was completely routed. Henry was pressing the siege of Terouanne and Tournay, when the events related in our ballad transpired in the northern marches of England. The fall of these two towns, and the defeat of the Scottish allies of France, brought about a truce and the submission of the French King, who married Mary Tudor, sister of the king of England, but died a few months after the marriage.

4.—FLODDON MOUNT.—"The eminence, called Floddon, lies near the river Till. It is the last and lowest of those hills, that extend on the north-east of the great mountain of Cheviot, towards the low ground on the side of the Tweed, from which river Floddon is distant about four miles. The ascent to the top of it, from the side of the river Till, where it takes a northerly direction, just by the foot of the declivity on which the castle and village of Ford stand, is about half a mile; and over the Till, at that place, there is a bridge. On the south of Floddon lies the extensive and very level plain of Millfield, having on its west side high hills, the branches of the Cheviot; on the north, Floddon, and other moderate eminences adjoining to it; on the south and east, a tract of rising grounds, nigh the foot of which is the slow and winding course of the Till. The nearest approach for the English army to Floddon was through this plain, in every part whereof they would have been in full view of the Scots, where they had a great advantage in possessing an eminence, which, on the side towards the English, had a long declivity, with hollow and marshy grounds at its foot, while its crown contained such an extent of almost level ground, as would have sufficed for drawing up, in good order, the forces that occupied it."—W. HUTCHINSON's *Northumberland.*

5.—THOMAS HOWARD, earl of Surrey, was the son of Sir John Howard, lord admiral of England, who fell at Bosworth field in 1485. He was knighted for his remarkable courage at the battle of Barnet, and made a knight of the Garter, 1 Rich. III. " He was taken prisoner in the battle of Bosworth, and committed to the Tower by Henry VII. and attainted by Parliament. King Henry asked him, How he durst bear arms in behalf of that tyrant Richard? to which he answered: 'He was my crowned king, and if the parliamentary authority of England set the crown upon a stock, I will fight for that stock; and as I fought then for him, I will fight for you, when you are established by the said authority.' In the rebellion against the King, by the Earl of Lincoln, the Lieutenant of the Tower offered the Earl of Surrey the keys of the Tower, in order to set himself at liberty; but he replied, 'That he would not be delivered by any power but by that which had committed him.' After he had been in prison three years and a half, the King gave him his liberty; and, knowing his worth and nice sense of honour, he took him into favour, and delivered up to him all his estates. The Earl took all occasions of relieving the oppressed subjects, and was accounted one of the ablest and greatest men in the kingdom. The Scots made an irruption into England, and besieged Norham Castle: the Earl raised the siege, took the castle of Ayton, and made all the country round a desert. James IV. of Scotland, incensed at this, sent a herald with a challenge to him, to which he made a sensible and spirited answer: 'That his life belonged to the King, whilst he had the command of his army; but when that was ended, that he would fight the King on horseback, or on foot: adding, that, if he took the King prisoner in the combat,

he would release him without any ransom; and that if the
King should vanquish him, he would then pay such a sum for
his liberty, as was competent for the degree of an Earl.' A. 1501,
the Earl was Lord High Treasurer. In June 1502, Margaret,
the King's daughter, a beautiful princess, at the age of fourteen
years, was attended by the Earl of Surrey, with a great company
of lords, ladies, knights, and squires, to the town of Berwick,
whence she was conveyed to St. Lambert's church, in Lamyr-
moor, where King James, attended by the chief nobility, received
her, and carried her to Edinburgh. The next day after her arri-
val there, she was, with great solemnity, married unto him, in
the presence of all his nobles. The King gave great entertain-
ments to the English, whom the Scotch noblemen and ladies far
out-shone, both in costly apparel, rich jewels, massy chains,
habiliments set with goldsmith's work, garnished with pearl, and
stones of price, and in gallant and well-trapped horses. They
made also great feasts for the English lords and ladies, and
shewed them jousting and other pleasant pastimes, as good as
could be devised, after the manner of Scotland. Diverse ladies
of Queen Margaret's train remained in Scotland, and were afterwards well married to noblemen."—LESLY, HOLINSHED.

" In 1507, two years before the death of Henry VII., the Earl
was appointed ambassador to the King of France. 2 Henry
VIII., he was made Earl Marshall for life. A. 1511, he was one
of the commissioners at the court of Arragon. When Henry
VIII. heard that the Scots were preparing to invade England,
he said, "That he had left a nobleman, who would defend his
subjects from insults." After the battle of Floddon, the Earl
himself presented King James's armour to the Queen-regent.
When the King returned from France, he gave the Earl an aug-
mentation of his arms, viz. to bear on the bend, the upper part
of a red lion, depicted in the same manner as the arms of Scotland, pierced through the mouth with an arrow. A. 1514, [the
first of February,] the Earl was created Duke of Norfolk, and a
grant was given him in special tail of several manors. He hated
and opposed Cardinal Wolsey, because he advised the King to
measures hurtful to the liberties of the people. Finding that
this opposition availed nothing, he resigned his post, and retired
from court. He died A. 1515, [the 21st May."]—LAMBE.

6.—SIR EDWARD STANLEY, the fifth son of Thomas, first Earl
of Derby, commanded the rear at the battle of Floddon, and,
with his Lancashire archers, forced the right wing of the Scots
from its advantageous position on the hill, and by this manœuvre

decided the battle. For these services, he was, the following year, created Lord Monteagle, because his ancestors bore an eagle for their crest. From the distinguished manner in which he is mentioned by our poet, celebrating his achievements above those of all the other English generals, particularly those of the Howard family, a close connection with the Stanleys may be inferred. The northern idioms which abound in this work joined to the above evidence, render it more than probable, that the author was a retainer, or at least under the influence of that family.—WEBER.

Sir Edward Stanley made a solemn declaration before he went to this battle, that if he returned victorious, he would do something to the honour of God; and accordingly, on his return, he began to build the magnificent chapel of Hornby; the steeple being an octagon of hewn stone, of an extensive height, with six bells; the chancel of the like stone, with diverse figures thereon, and the roof covered with lead. An eagle cut in stone, with an inscription in Roman text, "*Edwardus Stanley, Miles, Dominus Monteaglè, Me fieri fecit.*" He dying before it was perfected, the parish finished the body of the chapel, which is of inferior work.—BENSON.

7.—BISHOPRICK, i.e. the bishoprick of Durham.

8.—DACRES. The family of the Dacres of Gilsland, which is here spoken of, must not be mistaken for the Yorkshire Dacres. Thomas, lord Dacre of Gilsland, was one of the most active generals and wardens against Scotland. Notwithstanding the aspersions cast upon him by some enemies at court, against which he fully defends his conduct in a curious letter to the council, dated 1514, and printed from the original in Pinkerton's History of Scotland, he is spoken of in high terms in the original Gazette of Floddon-Field, by the Lord Admiral, who seems to have drawn up the account. As the whole passage strongly vindicates the warden's character, and, at the same time, the defeat of Sir Edmond Howard is candidly allowed, it shall be extracted at length:—"Item—Edmond Haward, second filz du Conte de Surrey, avoit avec luy mil hommes du pays de Lanqchere et Cheshire, et plusieurs autres gentilz hommes de la Conté d'York. Et faisoit le d'Edmond la droicte elle du seigneur de Haward son frere, surlequelz le seigneur Chambellan du Roy d'Ecosse, avec plusieurs autres srs. donnerent dedens. Maistre Gray, et Mesr Humfrey, demourent prisonnirs,, et Messire Richard Harbottell tué, et le d'Edmond Haward fut trois fois abatu; et vint a son relief le seigneur Dacres avec XVc hommes;

et tellement exploicta quil mist en fuyte le d'Escossois, et eut envyron ..., des gens dud. seigneur Dacres tuez, et en la d'bataille fut tué ung grant nombre des d'Escossois."

Lord Dacre accompanied, in 9 Henry VII., the Earl of Surrey in his expedition to the relief of Norham-castle. At the battle of Floddon he commanded the cavalry, and encountered the Earls of Huntley and Hume, where, of the Homes, Sir John, Cuthbert of Fastcastle, and many others were slain. In 1512, he accepted the office of Warden of the East and Middle Marches, which Lord Darcy had refused. He seems subsequently also to have had the West Marches under his control; and in the above-mentioned letter boasts of having destroyed six times more Scottish towns and houses, than the Scots had been able to burn. At the same time he accuses Lord Darcy, the Earl of Northumberland, the Bishop of Durham, and William Heron of Ford, of refusing to obey his summons. Besides his martial exploits, he carried on various negotiations, to the great advancement of English influence at the court of Scotland. —WEBER.

9 & 10.—LATHAM HOUSE. near Ormskirk, in Lancashire. "This family is originally from Cheshire, but removed hither upon this occasion. Sir John Stanley married the sole heiress of Sir Thomas Latham, and had with her this seat, and a large estate belonging to it; to which he, upon his marriage, removing, made many additions, that, with what his successors built afterwards, it became the principal seat of the family. This house is famous for a siege of two year's continuance, maintained by Charlotte, Countess of Derby, against the Parliament forces, who were forced to leave it untaken, though they afterwards became masters of it, and laid it almost level with the ground; the heroic lord of it being beheaded at Bolton, October 15, 1651."—BENSON.

11.—HENRY, LORD CLIFFORD, the "Shepherd Lord," was born in 1453, two years before the battle of St. Albans in which his grand-parent, Thomas Lord Clifford, was slain. This bereavement gave to John, the succeeding lord, cause for prosecuting with increased bitterness the part he had marked out for himself. But in 1461 he too fell, and thus in a time of unparalleled disquiet the youthful Henry, future lord of Skipton, was left, with a younger brother and sister, to the care of a defenceless mother. For the estates of John Lord Clifford, as of many other Lancastrian nobles, were at once seized by the king under an Act of Attainder. The mode adopted by Lady Clifford for preserving the young heir was a very ingenious one. When but seven years of age, while yet unable to comprehend the danger which threatened him, he was sent to Londesbrough, and given over to the charge of a shepherd, who clothed him and in every way treated him as his own child. He was subsequently sent, for greater safety, to Threlkeld, in Cumberland, where he remained for twenty-five years in concealment, living the life of a shepherd, till after the battle of Bosworth, when he was restored by Henry VII. to his honours, being then thirty-one years old, and unable to read. He was greatly attached to astronomy; and in order to indulge his propensity to that art, built Barden-tower, in Yorkshire, near the priory of Bolton ; for the canons of this house were great adepts at that science. He accompanied the Earl of Surrey in his expedition to Norham and Ayton castle. At Floddon-Field he bore a principal command. He died April 17, 1523. (See also Dawson's History of Skipton.)

12.—THOMAS STANLEY, first earl of Derby, was one of the chief supporters of Henry VII, in his endeavours to gain the crown of England. He built Greenhaugh Castle, near Garstang, in Lancashire, as a garrison for the king.

13.—HENRY, LORD SCROOP of Upsall, seventh baron, succeeded to the title in 1494 ; he was summoned to Parliament 28 November, 1511, and died without issue.

14.—THOMAS, second earl of Derby, is here alluded to. He succeeded his grandfather in the year 1504. He attended Henry VIII. in his expedition to Therouenne and Tournay in 1513, and died the 24th of May, 1522.

15.—SIR WILLIAM BULMER of Brumspeth castle. The last of this family, summoned as peer of the realm to parliament, was Ralph, from 1 till 24 Edward III. Sir William routed the borderers under Lord Home, who had made an incursion into England, previous to the battle of Floddon.

16.—HOUSE OF FENCE, see note on page 91.

17.—WAR IN FRANCE, see note 3, ante.

18.—JAMES IV., king of Scotland, was born 17 March, 1472, being the son of James III. by Margaret of Denmark. He was of an open and generous disposition, and obtained the affection of his people by his many good qualities. Successful in his early enterprises both by land and by sea, he entered into a treaty of amity and alliance with Henry VII. of England in 1503, the first after nearly 200 years of continual strife between Scotland and England. To make this treaty more binding, James married Margaret, sister of Henry VII. of England. After the death of the latter, in 1509, however, the relations between the two countries became less friendly, and in 1511, James demanded reparation for an outrage on the Scottish flag (for which see note 22, on Andrew Barton, below), which was contemptuously refused. The murder of Sir Robert Ker, (see note 25, on Scotch Warden, below), by some English Borderers, and the detention of queen Margaret's jewels, were further causes leading to the crisis which culminated in the disastrous battle of Floddon.

19.—The alleged homage of England to the crown of Scotland has no better foundation than the overrunning of the whole island by the Picts and Scots previous to the invasion of Britain by the Anglo-Saxons.

20.—DOUGLAS. The family of Douglas is the oldest and most celebrated of Scottish families. The first member of it of whom we have any direct record, is William of Douglas, who witnesses a royal charter in 1175. The Douglas alluded to in our ballad, is Archibald Douglas, surnamed "Bell-the-Cat," and also "the Great Earl," son of George, fourth earl of Angus, the "Red Douglas" who aided the king in his expedition against the "Black Douglasses." Archibald Douglas filled all the highest offices in the state, and died at Whithorn in Galloway in 1514. His grandson, also called Archibald, married Margaret of England, widow of James IV.

21.—SIR EDWARD HOWARD, son of Thomas Howard, and brother of Thomas, first created by Henry VIII. lord admiral of the fleet in consequence of the brilliant action related in the next note. He lost his life in 1513 in boarding a French vessel off Brest (see note 69).

22.—ANDREW BARTON. The reference here is to the battle which was fought in the year 1511, between a gallant Scottish mariner, Sir Andrew Barton, and Sir Thomas Howard and Sir Edward his brother, sons to the earl of Surrey, afterwards duke of Norfolk. Barton, it appears, having suffered both insult and loss from the Portuguese, fitted out two ships of war, by permission of James IV. of Scotland, to make reprisals, and such was his success that he enriched himself and became a terror of the seas. Under pretence of searching for Portuguese merchandise, he stopped and, it is added, pillaged some of the ships of England. This so exasperated Surrey, that he declared at the English council-board the narrow seas should not be so infested while he had an estate to furnish a ship and a son to command one. King Henry took Surrey at his word: two ships were fitted out at the earl's expense, and sent to sea under the command of his sons, with orders to intercept and capture Barton, which they were not the less willing to undertake, knowing that his ships were richly laden. The engagement which ensued was bloody and obstinate, and of long duration ; but the fortune of the Howards prevailed : Barton fell fighting valiantly ; his ships were carried into the Thames : the wealth obtained was large, and Sir Edward Howard was soon afterwards created Admiral of England. This act, committed in the time of peace, exasperated the Scots : Henry, to pacify them, liberated the crews; and offered to allow the aggrieved parties to prosecute their claims of restitution in the English courts of law.

23.—GELDERS. The long-standing quarrels between Henry VII. of England and the archduke Philip, duke of Burgundy and Gelderland, culminated in the ungenerous conduct of Henry, who, when Philip was driven by a tempest upon the shores of England, forced him to sign a humiliating treaty between England and Flanders.

24.—HERON. For the old Northumbrian family of Heron see the "Genealogical History of the Family of Heron" published in London, in 1803, from which we extract the following note referring to the Bastard Heron :—"John Heron, the bastard, was son of John Heron of Ford, by a concubine. Having in an affray at a border-meeting unfortunately killed Sir Robert Ker, warden of the middle marches, butler to James IV., and a great favourite with the King, he was outlawed in both kingdoms. Henry VII., to appease his son-in-law, delivered Sir William Heron to James, who kept him a prisoner in Fastcastle-Tower, in the Merse, on a rock above the Firth of Forth, until the battle of Floddon Field. In the first onset of the battle, the right wing of the English army was defeated, and Sir Edmund Howard, who commanded it, being left alone on the ground, the Bastard, at the head of a troop of horse he had disciplined in the Cheviot mountains, threw himself between the two armies, and engaged the enemy until the English rallied. Some accounts join Lord Dacre with the Bastard in this action ; but Hall, an author of great authority, says in his Chronicle, "that Heron, the bastard, though much wounded, rescued Sir Edmund ; and that Lord Dacre, wyth hys company, stode styl al day unfoughten withall." This is, however, disproved by Dacre's letter printed in Pinkerton's History, and by the original Gazette of the Lord Admiral. The Bastard, who was a famous warrior in those days, was afterwards killed, as some authors report, in an engagement on the Borders. He must have been older than his brothers ; for on the death of Sir Ralph Grey, the 4th April, 1506, Johis

Heron Bastardus was found to be seised of the manors of Chilt-
ingham, Howick, &c. &c. as surviving feoffee, in trust for Lady
Grey for life. It is therefore probable, the Bastard was born
before his father's marriage"

25.—MURDER OF THE SCOTCH WARDEN. Sir Robert Carr,
[Ker] was made by James IV. his chief butler, engineer, and
warden of the middle marches. He was much esteemed by the
King for his virtuous qualities. He was a severe punisher of the
English and Scotch Border-robbers, therefore they were deter-
mined to destroy him. At a solemn meeting between the English
and Scotch, [A. 1511.] in order to reclaim stolen goods, alterca-
tions arose, when three desperate Englishmen, John Heron the
Bastard, Lilburn, and Starhed, fell upon him; one of whom
stabbed him with a spear in the back, and the other two des-
patched him. Henry VII., enraged at this villanous action,
delivered William Heron, laird of Ford, brother to the Bastard,
and Lilburn, to the Scots, who imprisoned them in Fastcastle
tower in the Merse, where the latter died. The Bastard and
Starhed hid themselves in the interior parts of England, until
the reign of Henry VIII. when the Bastard, trusting to the
power of his relations, appeared openly at his own house, and
privately sent thieves into Scotland to disturb the peace. Starhed thought himself safe, having built himself a house at the
distance of ninety miles from the Border. But Andrew Carr,
the son of Robert, prevailed upon two of his dependants, of the
name of Tate, to disguise themselves, who entered Starhed's
house at night, and brought away his head to Andrew, who fixed
it in one of the most conspicuous places of the city of Edinburgh.

26.—MAXWELL, John, fourth lord Maxwell, fell at Flodden.

27.—LOUIS XII. of France, was born at Blois in 1462, son
of Charles, duke of Orleans, and Marie de Cleves. He was 36
years of age when he ascended the throne of France and succeeded to the rich heritage left to him by Louis XI. He devoted
all the resources of his kingdom to the attempted conquest of
Italy, and thereby rendered himself unable to cope successfully
with the powers who formed the coalition of Malines against
him. These powers, viz. Henry VIII. of England, the German
emperor Maximilian, Ferdinand of Castile, and the pope, sent
their troops to invade France in 1512, while Louis' sole ally,
James IV. of Scotland, who hoped to assist him by invading
England during Henry's absence in France, met with the
terrible disaster at Flodden which forms the subject of our
ballad : so that Louis XII. was obliged to purchase peace
by submitting to the conditions imposed by the victorious

coalition. These conditions, as far as England was concerned,
included the marriage of Louis with Mary, sister of Henry
VIII., and the payment of 100,000 crowns per annum for
ten years to the English monarch. Louis, however, died a
few months after the marriage, on the 1st of January, 1515,
in his fifty-third year.

28.—BERWICK-ON-TWEED, for a long time a county of itself,
and now an integral part of Northumberland, formerly belonged
undoubtedly to the realm of Scotland. It was frequently taken
and re-taken by the English and the Scots, but in 1482 passed
finally into the permanent possession of the English, by whom
it was strongly garrisoned at the time of the battle of Floddon.

29.—HUME. Alexander, third Lord Hume, succeeded his father
in 1506. He was a man of great abilities, and was promoted
by James IV. to the office of Lord High Chamberlain, in the
end of 1507. While this sovereign lived, he continued in high
favour. Previous to the battle of Floddon, he made, probably
by order of the King, an inroad into England, but was defeated
by Sir William Bulmer, and the prey he had collected taken
from him. Nothwithstanding the calumnies of historians, who
went so far as to accuse him of murdering his sovereign subsequently to the battle, it appears that he fought with great
bravery. He continued in favour during the minority of James
V.; till his opposition to Albany having caused his exile, he
imprudently returned, and, being tried and convicted of treason
before the parliament of Scotland, he was beheaded Oct. 8, 1516.

30.—DELLAMOUNT. It has been attempted to identify this
personage with Sir David Lindsay "of the Mount," who was
Lyon-king-at-arms in 1530, *i.e.* seventeen years after the battle
(see Notes & Queries 5th S.x. 221, 473). There is not a
particle of evidence, however, to show that a Scottish Lyon-king
is referred to in this stanza; on the contrary, the expression
"Dellamount who bodword out of France did bring," can only
denote a special messenger sent by the king of France, to
request the aid of the Scottish King against England. Delmont,
Délémont, Delamont, are still surnames common enough in
France; moreover, the fact of this personage being a foreigner
becomes clear from his describing the leaders of the English
army by their banners and coats-of-arms, whilst his hearers, viz.
king James and the Scottish nobles, identify them one after
another from his description. Had Dellamount been a Scottish
Lyon-king, he would certainly have been far more likely to know
their names than his hearers did. It will be superfluous to ask
how our Craven author could become acquainted with the fact

of Sir David Lindsay's being Scottish Lyon-king, in 1530, during the time of almost complete cessation of intercourse which followed the events related in our ballad.

31.—HERBERT. Charles, natural son of Henry, Duke of Somerset, and a man of great abilities, was constituted in 1509 one of the privy council, and acquired the title of Lord Herbert, by his marriage with Elizabeth, heiress of William Herbert, Earl of Huntingdon. He had summons to the parliaments in 1509 and 1511 among the barons, by the name of Charles Somerset de Herbert Chevalier. He attended Henry VIII. with 6000 foot to Therouenne and Tournay; and, for his valour, received the office of Lord Chamberlain for life, and the title of Earl of Worcester. He died in the year 1525, and was buried in St. George's Chapel, Windsor.

32.—PIERCY. Henry Percy, fifth Earl of Northumberland, succeeded his father, who was murdered by the rebels, as Lieutenant of Yorkshire, in 4 Henry VII. In the battle of Blackheath, against Lord Audley and his followers, he was one of the chief commanders. In 1513 he accompanied Henry VIII. to Therouenne, and died A. 1525.

33.—SHREWSBURY. George Talbot, Earl of Shrewsbury, succeeded his father, who died September 26th, 1464. In 1487, he fought at the battle of Stoke, near Newark, against the rebels, and, three years after that, was sent with others to Flanders, to the aid of the emperor Maximilian. In 1513, he commanded the vanguard of the king's army at Therouenne. He made some inroads into Scotland, as lieutenant of the north, in 1522; and in 1537 marched as the King's lieutenant to quell the insurrection in Yorkshire, called the Pilgrimage of Grace. He died July 26th, 1542.

34.—DARCY. Thomas, Lord Darcy, succeeded William in 1497. In the same year he marched with Thomas, Earl of Surrey, to the relief of Norham castle. In 1498, being made a knight of the King's body, he was made constable of the castle of Bambrough, and, in the ensuing year, captain of the town and castle of Berwick; also warden of the East and Middle Marches. In 1502, he was one of the commissioners to receive the oath of James IV., on a treaty of peace. He was appointed general warden of the marches towards Scotland in 1506, and served two campaigns in the wars of Ferdinand of Arragon against the Moors, in 1510 and 1511. The 20th of June, 1539, he was beheaded for delivering up Pontefract castle to Robert Aske, commander of the rebels assembled on account of religious differences in the north.

35.—DUDLEY. Edward, Lord Dudley, Knight of the Garter, was summoned to Parliament from 1492 to 1530.

36.—DELAWARE. Thomas West, Lord La Warre, succeeded his father in 16 Edward IV. He died 9th October, 1554.

37.—DRUERY. For a full pedigree of the Drury family, see "History and Antiquities of Hawsted and Hardwick," by the Rev. Sir John Cullum, Knt., London, 1813.

38.—BUCKINGHAM. Edward Stafford, Duke of Buckingham, succeeded his father, who was executed for rising in arms against Richard III. He was one of the commanders against the Cornishmen in 13 Henry VII. Shortly before his fall, the splendour of his appointment was greater than that of any other nobleman. He was ruined by the knavery of Knivet, a steward whom he had discharged for his tyranny against his tenants; and by the enmity and envy of Wolsey. He was beheaded May 17th, 1521.

39.—COBHAM. Thomas Brooke, Lord Cobham, succeeded his father in 1506. He was with Henry VIII. at Therouenne and Tournay, and the following year was sent with Lord Abergavenny to Calais. He died the 19th July, 1521.

40.—WILLOUGHBY. Sir John Willoughby, of Middleton in the county of Warwick married one of the sisters of John Grey, viscount Lisle. In the church at Middleton there are many monuments to this family.

41.—ESSEX. Henry Bouchier, Earl of Essex, succeeded 1483. In 1 Henry VII. he was one of the privy council, and A. 1493 attended that King to the siege of Boulogne. Four years after he was one of the chief commanders at Blackheath, against the Cornish insurgents. In 1509 he was appointed by Henry VIII. captain of his horseguard. In 1513, he was at Therouenne and Tournay, being then Lieutenant General of all the king's spears. He was killed by a fall from his horse, A. 1540.

42.—STAFFORD. Henry Stafford, created 1508 Earl of Wiltshire. He died without issue, March 6th, 1522.

43.—GRAY. Richard de Grey, Earl of Kent, Knight of the Garter, attended Henry VIII. to Therouenne, and died the 3rd of May, 1524.

44.—HASTINGS. George, Lord Hastings, succeeded 1507, and attended Henry VIII. to Therouenne in 1513. He was created Earl of Huntingdon in 1530; and in 1537 marched with other lords against the Pilgrimage of Grace. He died the 24th of March, 1554.

45.—DORSET. Thomas Grey, Marquis of Dorset, succeeded his father in 18 Henry VII. In 1311 he was general of the troops sent to Spain. In 1513, he and four of his brothers, with some other English gentlemen, attended the tournament proclaimed at St. Denis, by Francis de Valois, heir of the crown of France. At the meeting of Henry VIII. and Francis I., he carried the sword of the former. He died A. 1530.

46.—FITZWATER. Robert Radcliffe, Lord Fitzwalter, having borne arms for Percy Warbeck, was attainted. After his death the son was restored by Henry VII. in 1506, to his honours. He was at the siege of Therouenne and Tournay. In 1523, he led the van in Surrey's expedition into France; and in 1526, was created Viscount Fitzwalter for his services, and the 28th September, 1529, Earl of Sussex. He was appointed Lord High Chancellor of England for life, and died October 17, 1542.

48.—Hume of Loudon, see note 29.

49.—SIR JOHN NEVIL, grandson of Ralph, lord Nevil, of Raby Castle and earl of Westmoreland.

50.—LYON-KING, at the period of the battle of Floddon, was Sir William Cumyng of Inverallochy, second son of William Cumyng of Coulter who was Marchmont herald in 1499.

51.—TERWIN. Terouanne, in Picardy, near St. Omer, in the department of Pas de Calais.

52. HARRAD is Harewood, in Yorkshire, the history and antiquities of which were written by John Jones; London: Simpkin, Marshall & Co., 1859.

53.—JUDGE GASCOIGNE. Sir William Gascoigne was born in 1350, at Gawthorp, near Harewood. He studied at Cambridge, entered Gray's Inn, and rapidly rose in favour at court. He was appointed chief justice in 1401. His committal of Henry V. to prison while yet Prince of Wales, for striking him while on the seat of justice, is immortalized in Shakespeare's Henry IV. He retired from public life in 1413, and died in 1419.

54.—RUDIMOND. Sir Richard Redman, knight, son of John de Redman, of Cumberland and Yorkshire, married Elizabeth, co-heiress of Sir William de Aldburgh, of Harewood Castle, He died in 1423, and was interred in Harewood church where a splendid recumbent monument perpetuates his memory.

54a.—SIR PHILIP TILNEY, of a family long settled in Suffolk and Norfolk. His daughter Agnes became the second wife of the earl of Surrey who commanded at Floddon,

55.—Sir Richard Appleyard, of Burstwick Garth in Holderness.

57.—Alexander Stuart, archbishop of St. Andrews, natural son of James IV., by Margaret, daughter of Archibald Boyd of Bonshaw, was born in 1495. His father loaded him with honours political and ecclesiastical though but a youth.

58.—St. Andrew. The diocese of St. Andrews was under the invocation of Andrew, the apostle, brother of Peter.

59.—Trimon of Quitorn. St. Ninian's of Withorn, a celebrated shrine in Galloway, visited by high and low in mediæval times. The festival of St. Ninian was on the 16th September.

60.—Doffin. Duthack, Bishop and confessor, lived at Tain in Ross-shire. His festival fell on the 31st August.

61.—Norham Castle was built against the inroads of the Scottish borderers, by Ranulph Flamberg, bishop of Durham, in 21 Henry I. Henry Puteal, one of his successors, built the great tower in 1180. The Scots having destroyed it, bishop Hugh Pudsey rebuilt it in the reign of king Stephen. Edward I. called a Parliament to Norham in 1291, and received there the formal acknowledgment by the Scottish lords of his sovereignty over Scotland.

62.—St. Cuthbert of Durham, one of the great saints of England, was born about 635, of humble parents. A vision which he had in 651, when watching his flock, induced him to enter monastic life at Melrose. He became successively prior of Lindisfarne, an anchorite on Farne Island, abbot of Lindisfarne, and bishop of Hexham, and finally died as an anchorite on the 20th March, 687.

63.—Sir Marmaduke Constable of Flamborough, knt., was born in the year 1441. He had four sons; but how many of them attended him to the Field of Floddon, we are not able to determine. They were all knighted; the eldest, Sir Robert, on the 17th of June, A.D. 1497, at the battle of Blackheath. The others were, Sir Marmaduke, of Everingham; Sir William Constable, of Hatfield in Holderness, and Sir John Constable of Kinalton. Sir Robert having been active in the rising about religion, in 28 Henry VIII., was pardoned, but being again implicated in the revolt of Lord Hussey, and others, was attainted, and executed at Hull. His son, Marmaduke, attended Henry VIII. to Terouenne, and was knighted at Lille the 14th October, 1513.

67.—Sir Bryan Tunstall's effigy, in full proportion, cut in stone, lies over his body in the chancel of Tunstal Church

(Holderness). His residence was at Thurland Castle, in Lancashire.

68 and 69.—See notes 5 and 21.

70.—BARTHRUMB'S BAY, or Conquête Harbour. Sir Edward Howard, second son of the Earl of Surrey, Lord Admiral of England, appeared before Brest Harbour with forty-two vessels, and challenged the French fleet to combat. But the latter waited for reinforcements, which soon appeared, commanded by Prejeant de Bidoux. The gallant Admiral, however, would not await the junction of the fleet, but attacked it in Conquête harbour. He was the first who boarded the Admiral's ship, having rowed up with two gallies, filled with officers; and was followed by one Carroz, a Spanish cavalier, and seventeen Englishmen. The French meanwhile cut the cable; and Howard continuing to fight, was pushed overboard by the pikes, and drowned. The fleet, upon his death, returned to England.

71.—KING RICHARD'S FEILD, *i.e.*, the battle of Bosworth.

73.—SIR DAVID HALL was one of the chief supporters of the Duke of York, and strongly dissuaded him from leaving the safe shelter of Sandal Castle to meet the superior forces of Queen Margaret. He fell at the battle of Wakefield.

74.—JOHN, DUKE OF BEDFORD, third son of Henry IV. of England, was born in 1389. He was governor of Berwick and warden of the Scottish marches. After the death of his brother, Henry V., he went to France as regent, and defeated the French in various battles. The fight alluded to in this stanza, is the battle of Verneuil, in 1424, when the dauphin was disastrously routed. He died 19th September, 1435.

75.—TALBOT, see note 33.

76.—THE RAGING BOAR was the symbol of the earl of Warwick.

77.—MALCOLM III., king of Scotland, was killed at a place called Malcolm's well, near Alnwick, in 1092.

78.—KING DAVID II, (David Bruce), son of king Robert Bruce lost 15,000 men at the battle of Neville's Cross, in 1346, and was himself taken prisoner and shut up in the Tower of London. He was ransomed in 1357 for 10,000 marks, and died at Edinburgh, 22nd February, 1371.

79.—This battle was fought the 14th September, 1402, at Hamildon, in Northumberland.

80.—Ralph, third baron Ogle, was summoned to parliament in 1508 and 1511; his son Robert was summoned 23rd November, 1514, so that Ralph cannot have survived the battle long.

81.—HAUTON HILLS, the upper part of Litton Dale, with Halton Gill.

82.—John, lord Lumley, and Richard Nevil, lord Latimer; the latter died in 1530.

83.—WILLIAM CONYERS, son of Sir John Conyers by Margery, second daughter and co-heir of baron Philip Darcy. He died in 1524.

84.—BLACKAMOOR, the upper part of Nidderdale.

86.—SIR WALTER GRIFFIN, of an ancient Cheshire family. His residence was at Bartherton, near Nantwich.

87.—SIR JOHN EVERINGHAM de Wadsley was High Sheriff for the County of York in 1512. He resided at Everingham Park, near Pocklington.

88.—SIR CHRISTOPHER WARD, of Grindall, near Bridlington, was standard-bearer to Henry VIII. at Rouen. The original family seats were at Brereton and Scotton.

89.—MARTIN SWART, or Schwartz, a German colonel serving under John, Earl of Lincoln, was defeated by Henry VII., at Stoke, near Newark.

90.—SIR RICHARD BOLD, of Bold, in Lancashire, married the daughter of Sir Thomas Gerard, of Brindall.

91.—SIR THOMAS BUTLER, of Warrington, married Margaret, daughter of John Delves, of Doddington, in Cheshire. He died in 1523.

92.—RICHARD CHOLMONDELEY, of Cholmondeley, in Cheshire, was knighted in 12 Henry VII., for his services against Perkin Warbeck; and, at the battle of Floddon, commanded the forces of the town of Kingston upon Hull. For his achievements in this victory he was made lieutenant of the Tower of London. He died in the year 1521.

93.—HENRY, LORD SCROPE, of Bolton, married Alice, sole daughter and heiress of Thomas Scrope, of Upsall, thus uniting for a time the two branches of the Scrope family, viz., from 1493 to 1501.

94.—KIDSON CAUSEY.—See note 42, on page 108.

95.—SIR WILLIAM GASCOIGNE, son of Sir William Gascoigne, of Gawthorpe, by Margaret, daughter of Richard Nevil, lord Latimer.

96.—The family of STAPYLTON, which settled at Myton, in the time of Charles I., formerly resided at Carleton and Wighill.

97.—MARKENFIL. Sir Ninian Markenfield of Markenfield Hall, Markington, near Ripon. The estate became forfeited to the crown in 1569, Sir Thomas Markenfield having joined in the rebellion in the North.

98.—MAUNDEVILL.—Sir John Normanville led five hundred men from the city and ainsty of York at Floddon.

99.—SIR GUY DAWNAY,, ancestor of the present viscount Downe. DAWBY, probably refers to Sir Christopher Danby, who was knighted after the battle.

100.—RICHARD TEMPEST. His family has been seated for some centuries at Broughton Hall, near Skipton.

101.—JAMES JOHNSTON, lord of Johnston, succeeded his father in 1509, and died in 1528.

102.—The Musgraves are an old border family, settled on both sides of the Cheviots.

103.—SIR MALKIN KERNE, Sir Malcolm McKean.

104.—John Lindsay, fifth earl of Crawford, succeeded his father in 1494.

105.—William, Lord Graham, became earl of Montrose in 1504.

106.—William, second earl of Caithness, succeeded in 1408. David, Lord Kennedy and earl Cassilis, was a member of James' privy council.

107.—ARELL, William Hay, fifth earl of Errol. ATHELL, John Stewart, second earl of Athol, succeeded in 1512. Patrick Hepburn, third lord Hales, was created earl of BOTHWELL in 1438. GLENKARR, Cuthbert Cunningham, third earl of Glencairn.

108.—LOVAT, Thomas Fraser, the master of Lovat. CLUESTON, Sir Patrick Houston of Houston. INDERBY, Thomas Stewart, lord Innermeath. Ross, Sir John Ross Halkhead.

109.—ARSKILL, Robert, lord Erskine, and earl of Mar.

110.—SENTCLEAR, Henry Sinclair, lord Sinclair. SIMPELL, Sir John Semple, eighth baron of Eliotstoun, was created lord Semple in 1488.

111.—CADDIE HUME, Sir Cuthbert Hume of Fastcastle.

112.—HABURN.—For Hepburn, lord Bothwell, see note 107.

CRAVEN MEN

AT THE

𝕭attle of 𝕱lodden 𝕱ield.

Taken *from the Battle Roll at Bolton Abbey, in the possession of His Grace the Duke of Devonshire.*

KEIGHLEY.

John Rawson, bow, able-body horse, &c.	
Thomas Sowden,	bille
Willian Butterfield,	bow
Xrofer Ruddyng,	,,
John Shaw,	,,
John Brigg,	bille
John Stott,	bowe
Thomas Lakok,	bille
John Cockrofte,	bowe
Robert Wright,	,,
Robert Wright, junr.	,,
Willian Hartley,	,,
Willian Estburn,	bille
Law' Ambler, bow, able-body horse, &c.	
Richd. Try Hyll,	bowe
Robert Hudson,	,,
John Sugden,	,,
Richard Sharpe,	,,
John Widdoppe,	,,
Ellis Hall,	,,
John Butterfield,	bill
Richard Rycroft,	,,
John Netherwood,	bill
Edward Rawson,	bowe
Robert Bottomley,	,,
Richard Shaw,	,,
Thomas Stotte,	,,
Richard Jenkinson,	,,
Willian Denby,	bille
Willian Sugden,	,,
John Clough,	,,
William Smith,	,,
Robert Lupton,	,,
Ellis Wadsworth,	,,
William Roper,	,,
William Farnill,	,,
Robert Stelle,	,,
William Jackson,	bowe
John Hanson,	,,
Robert Rawson,	,,
Edward More,	,,
Richard Shackyton,	,,
James Procter,	,,
Robert Sugden,	,,
John Oldfield,	,,
John Weddope,	,,
Henry Beanlands,	,,

MARTON FOR MOSTER'S.

William Marton, a bow, horse, and harnish
Nickolas Synson, a bowe, horse, and harnish
Thomas Stockdale, a bille, horse, and harnish
Robert Stockdale, a bille, horse, and harnish
John Roberts,   a bowe
Richard Arnald,   ,,
John Tomlynson, able person and bille
Richard Bulcock, able person and bille
Robert Rossendale, a bill
To be hors'd and harnish'd at the town's cost.
Thos. Midopp, able person, horse and harnish'd
John Malham, able person, horse and harnish'd
Xrofer Styrke, able person, horse and harnish'd
John Swyer, junr., able person
Wm. Robert, able person

GERSYNTON.

John Clerk, a bow, able, horse and harnish'd
John Wilkinson,   a bowe
George Knolle,   ,,
Lennard Hibotson,   ,,

HAWKGSWYK.

William Calvard, a bow, able, horse and harnish'd
Athur Redyman, a bow, able, horse and harnish'd

ADYNGHAM.

William Wade, able, horse and harnish'd
Henry Man,   a archer
Richard Cryer,   ,,
Richard Riley,   ,,
Richard Lofthouse,   a bille
Thomas Stotte,   a archer
Christopher Swyer,   ,,
Thomas Barker,   ,,
John Greene,   ,,
The above hors'd and harnish'd at the town's cost.

ARNECLIFFE.

John Knolle, able, horse and harnish'd
Oliver Knolle,   a bowe
Robert Tylson,   a bill

FLASBY.

William Hessfell'd, a man, horse and harnish'd
Richard Lister,   a bille
William Blackborne,   ,,
Stephen Proctor, a man, hors'd, &c.
Rauffe Proctor, a man, hors'd, &c.
Rodger Proctor,   a bill
Lyonel Whitfield,   ,,
Robt. Snelle, hors'd and harnish'd

LYTTONDALE.

John Knolle, able, horse and harnish'd
Abraham Knolle,   bille
Richard Franklin,   bowe
Richard Fawcytt,   ,,
John Franklin,   ,,
Jack Tylson,   ,,

SETTYLL.

Richard Brown, a bow, able, horse, &c.
William Tayler,   a bowe
Oliver Foster,   ,,
Richard Cokeson,   ,,
William Knolle,   ,,
Adam Brown,   a bille
Rogr. Yveson,   a bowe
Rawlyn Lawson,   ,,
Allen Procter,   a bille
Henry Hoelson,   bow
Richard Carr,   ,,

GLOSEBORNE.

William Mayncond,   bowe, able, horse, &c.
Robert Summerscale,   bowe

LANGSTROTHDALE.

Richard Tenant, a bow, able, horse, &c.
Geoffery Tenant,   a bowe
John Tenant,   ,,
Thomas Slinger,   a bowe
Lenard Jake,   ,,
William Tenant,   ,,

GIGRESWYCK.

Robert Stakhouse, bow, able, horse, &c.
John Webster,   a bowe
Thos. Palay,   ,,
James Carr,   ,,
Thomas Browne,   a bille
Jack Stackhouse,   a bowe

STONEFOKD.

James Foster, bowe, able, horse, &c.
Adam Palay,   bowe
Robert Twistleton,   ,,
Richard Franklyn,   ,,
Richard Chew,   ,,
James Armisted,   a bille

LANGCLYFF.

Richard Brown, bow, able, horse, &c.
Rogr. Yveson,   a bowe
Henry Pacock,   a bill

THORLEBY.

Wm. Brochden, bill, able, horse, &c.
Robert Burgess,   a bille
Thomas Bacock,   ,,

EMBSAY AND ESTBY.

Thomas Alcock, bow, able, horse, &c.
Thomas Croft,   a bowe
William Cate, of Estby, a bille
John Pety,   do.   a bowe

HALTON.

Robert Burley, a bowe, able, horse, &c.
Francis Shyers,   a bowe
William West,   ,,

CEOLLYNG.

Pers. Tyllotson, a bow, able horse, &c.
Xrofer Lakok,   a bowe
Nicoles Starburgh   ,,
Henry Waller,   ,,

SUTTON.

John Blakay, bow, able, horse, &c.
John Parkinson

STEETON.

Richard Garford, a bow, able, horse, &c.
John Garford,   a bowe
John Parkinson,   a bille
John Whetaker's,   a bowe
William Smith,   ,,

William Eastburn,   a bille
Stephen Tyllotson, bow, able,
  horse, &c.
Thos, Smyth, junr.,   bowe

KILDWICK.

John Garford, bow, able,
  horse, &c.
Edward Garford,   bowe
Richard Herreson,   a bille

ESHETON.

Thos. Marton, a bow, able,
  horse, &c.

BEAMSLEY.

John Holmes, bow, able,
  horse, &c.
Thos. Frankland,   a bowe
Richard Shyers,   a bill
Thos. Kendal,   bill, able,
  horse, &c.

APPLETREWYCK.

Henry Young, bow, able,
  horse, &c.
William Wat,   a bowe
William Hog,   a bille
Thomas Preston,   a bowe
Robert Elston,   ,,
Cuthbt. Wynterb'n,   a bowe
Henry Young, bille & bowe

BRADLEY.

William Smith, bow, able,
  horse, &c.
Thomas, Slys,   bowe
Thomas Greenwood   ,,
Xrist. Smyth   ,,

FARNHYLL.

Henry Currer, bowe, able,
  horse, &c.

Edward Sally,   a bowe
Robert Bradley   ,,
William Wylson,   ,,

BOLTON-IN-BOLLAND.

William Stott, bow, able,
  horse, &c.
Henry Garnett,   a bowe
Robert Caley,   ,,
Thomas Pele,   bille

MORTON BANKS.

John Rogerson, a bow, able,
  horse, &c.
Richard Holymake,   a bowe
William Butterfield,   ,,

RYMINGTON.

Henry Burclay, bow, able,
  horse, &c.
Henry Arthynton,   bowe
James Oddy,   ,,
John Ray,   ,,

HELIFIELD AND NEWTON.

John Carr, bowe, able, horse,
  &c.
John Clark,   a bylle
John Hardaker,   a bowe
Thomas Badsby,   ,,

CARLTON.

Robert Tempest, bowe, able,
  horse, &c.
Robert Dawtree,   bowe
John Thompson,   ,,
Henry Wallkynson,   ,,
Richard Scarburgth,   ,,
Richard Stapylton,   ,,
John Smith,   ,,
William Throp,   ,,
Thomas Midybrok,   ,,
James Smith,   ,,
John Rycroft,   ,,

SETTYLLE.

Richard Tenant,	bille
Alan Proctor,	,,
Edward Lawson,	,,
Adam Browne,	bowe
Oliver Taleyor,	,,
Thomas Summerscale,	bille
William Symson,	,,
Robert Taleyor,	,,
John Watkynson,	,,
William Lawson,	,,
William Carr,	,,
Robert Midoppe,	,,
Richard Lund,	bowe
Richard Jackson,	,,
Roger Carr,	bowe
Hugh Carr,	,,
William Taleyor,	,,
Gyles Cokeson,	,,
George Hokison,	,,
John Holson,	,,
Richard Lawson,	,,

LYTTONDALE.

Adam Langstroth,	a bille
James Knolle,	,,
Rauffe Knowle,	,,
Matthew Knolle,	,,
William Thorneton,	,,
Jak Ellison,	,,
Roger Franklin,	bowe
Robert Stoneford,	bille
Henry Bullok,	,,
Henry Franklyn,	bowe
John Walker,	,,
Rodger Tenant,	,,
Thomas Wederheide,	,,
Jakob Tenant,	bille
Henry Tylson,	bowe
John Coward,	bille

ARNECLYFF.

William Firth,	bowe
Richard Clebenger,	bille

Peter Prass,	bille
John Carlyll,	,,
Richard Atkinson,	bowe
John Wilson,	,,
John Atkinson,	,,

LANGSTROTH.

Rauffe Tenant,	bowe
James Parker,	,,
William Langstroth,	,,
Geffery Walker,	,,
Thomas Tenant,	,,
Adam Wilkynson,	bille
John Faldshaw,	bowe
Xrofer Hogg,	,,
Richard Smyth,	,,
James Case,	,,
Xrofer Slyng,	bille

STONEFORD.

Adam Valay	bille
Roger Lawson,	,,
Roger Swaynson,	bowe
Richard Palay,	,,
James Armested,	bille
John Hokeson,	bowe
Oliver Armsted,	,,
Henry Lawkland,	,,
Willian Foster,	bill
John Yveson,	,,
Roger Yveson,	,,

GYGRESWYCK.

Richard Brayshay,	bowe
Richard Wilson,	,,
Robert Burron,	bille
John Brayshay,	bowe
Thomas Tayleyor,	,,
Thomas Preston,	,,
John Stakhouse,	bowe
Willian Ryley,	,,
Thomas Armested,	,,
John Taleyor,	,,

Henry Tayleor,   bowe
Thomas Newhouse   ,,
Oliver Stakhouse,   ,,
Henry Armested,   ,,

LANGECLYFF.

Robert Kydson,   bille
Richard Kyng,   ,,
Robert Kydd,   ,,
William Yveson,   ,,
John Stakhouse,   ,,
Roger Browne,   bowe

MORTON BANKS.

Willian Rogerson,   bowe
John Fuller,   bill
Willian Leche,   ,,
John Leche,   ,,
Willian Sharppe,   bowe
William Adamson,   bill
Edmond Dobson,   ,,
Adam Wodde,   ,,

BOLTON-BY-BOLLAND.

Humphrey Pickard,   bowe
Thomas Pykhard,   ,,
John Wyglesworth,   ,,
John Garrett,   bille
Richard Calmers,   bowe
Thomas Foot,   ,,
Robert Walbank,   ,,
William Knott,   bille
Willian Catley,   bowe

HELYFELD AND NEWTON.

Thomas Wray,   bowe
Henry Carr,   ,,
William Forte,   bylle
Thos. Hardaker,   ,,
Roger Hardaker,   bowe

RYMINGTON.

Robert Calmley,   bowe
Robert Tattersall,   bylle
Richard Hoghton,   bowe
Thomas Walar,   bylle
Robert Calmley, junr.,   bowe
William Carr,   ,,
Gyles Lodge,   ,,
Robert Forte,   ,,
Christr. Pykhard,   ,,
Thomas Land,   bille
Roger Land,   ,,
Robert Dansar,   bowe
Christr. Hornby,   ,,
Richard Walar,   bylle

CARLTON.

Richard Scarburgh,   bowe
Richard Stapylton,   ,,
John Smith,   ,,
Willian Thorp,   ,,
Thomas Midybrok,   ,,
James Smith,   ,,
John Rycroft   ,,

J. S. Toothill, Printer, &c., 93, Upper Godwin Street, Bradford.